LOVE COMES TO BLUEBONNET INN

An American State Flower novella

By Martha Rogers

ISBN-13: 978-1530704859
ISBN-10: 1530704855

1 CHAPTER NAME

Chapter 1

*W*hy had she returned to her boring home town? Jolie Burns slumped in a rocking chair on the porch of Bluebonnet Inn and Tearoom. As much as she loved her mother and the Inn, Weinberg, Texas was a boring little town, and one she'd fled as soon as she'd graduated college. Nothing had gone right from the moment she answered her mother's plea for help last spring to this moment sitting alone on the porch of the Bluebonnet Inn, almost a year later.

Her decision had cost her engagement to an up-and-coming young man with high political hopes. Seems he wanted her by his side at all times, showing off her ring, but never truly settled on a wedding date. Four months ago she learned he had a new woman at his side on his campaign trail for state representative.

Moving back here had ended her social life and brought it to a complete standstill. All her old friends from high school but one were married with families or had moved away. As for men, forget that. The pickings in Weinberg were nada, zilch. The ones around her age had long left for the greener pastures in Dallas or Houston. But then, she wasn't ready for another relationship now anyway.

Despite the sunny but mild spring weather, her favorite time of the year, Jolie wished for something to make her days more meaningful even though she now realized how much better off she was without Mark Hartley.

Tired of rocking, Jolie shifted from the chair to the old porch swing and shoved off with her toe. Mondays were the worst. All the weekend guests had checked out, and Mom entertained her girlfriends after their Monday morning Bible study and prayer time.

Conversation and laughter filtered through the window and to the porch where she sat swinging. At least Mom and her friends enjoyed themselves on this early April morning. Usually the sight of the bluebonnets coming into bloom thrilled her heart, but today they simply increased her loneliness.

The sign near the street, declaring this to be the *Bluebonnet Inn: Bed and Breakfast and Tearoom* creaked in the gentle wind that hinted of the spring weather. Two events loomed ahead before the summer season launched, and the inn was booked solid for both. The annual Bluebonnet Fair drew people to the hill country town in droves to sample the wares of local crafts people and merchants of all kinds. Then the first weekend in June, the Founder's Day Festival and Antique Show drew patrons from all across Texas.

After all the problems they'd faced during the remodeling before the grand opening last Labor Day weekend, she and Mom finally found the books in the black with reservations for the fair and fall festival. The hustle and bustle of luring patrons and planning meals and activities had filled Jolie's days for the past ten months, and now the tearoom did a brisk business four days a week. Except for the lack of a social life, she did enjoy helping her mother make a success of the inn.

She tucked her feet up under her legs and gazed out at the street. Mom had done a wonderful job with the design and layout for turning their old Victorian home into a bed and breakfast, but the summer months may well see more empty rooms than full because of the Texas heat. People with good sense chose cooler climates for vacation.

Charlene Sanders's laugh echoed across the porch and Jolie smiled. Mom's best friend had a laugh like no one else. Now that was one sassy, Southern woman for sure. Widowed around the same time as Mom, Charley had no fear in voicing her opinion about anything and everything, but she also bore a heart of gold and would practically lay down her life for Mom, or any of her friends for that matter.

The mailman ambled up the walk to the porch. "Howdy, Miss Jolene. Here's the mail." He held a stack of envelopes toward her.

She reached for them and smiled. "Thanks, Mr. Murray."

He nodded. "You're welcome, and tell your mom the missus and I are planning to have lunch here on Friday. That's her chicken pot pie day, and we don't want to miss it."

Jolie laughed and waved as he backed down the steps. "I will. I kinda like that pot pie myself."

The door opened, and the ladies from the Bible study spilled out to the porch, all chattering like magpies.

Charley's voice rose above the rest. "Well, I still think we need some excitement in this here town."

Excitement? Jolie shook her head. If something wasn't happening around town, Charley wanted to make it happen.

Mom wrapped her arm around Charley's shoulder. "Oh, pooh, we've had enough stuff for a while. With the Bluebonnet Fair around the corner, we'll be busy getting our crafts ready for our Bible class booth."

"That's not excitement in my book, but what can you expect in a town like ours."

"I'm content for things to run smoothly for a while. This inn and the tearoom will be around as long as I can keep it running."

Her mother's words had gained more confidence than she had when they first started the re-model on their old home. Making a profit did make a difference.

"Humph, y'all can sit around and drink tea and eat cookies all you want, but I'm getting bored. We need to find something else to do to stir up this town."

Mom's laughter at Charley's comments brightened Jolie's heart. Her mother was truly happy and had a new love interest in her life since Andy Benefield had moved back to Weinberg. That's all that was important.

The other two women with Mom and Charley laughed and patted their friend on the arm as they walked down the steps. Both waved at Jolie before heading for their cars.

Charley remained on the porch. "What are you doing out here, Jolie? Why didn't you come in and have tea with us?"

"Oh, I thought I'd sit out here and wait for the mail." Not exactly the truth, but then she saw no need to share with Charley the problems of having no social life.

Charley planted her hands on her hips, and Jolie braced herself for what was sure to come. "Seems to me you'd be out and about with your friends. Sitting on the porch, waiting for the mail is no activity for a pretty young thing like you." She turned and shook her finger at Mom. "See, that's why we need something exciting for this town. Nothing exciting has happened since that fire in your kitchen during remodeling."

Jolie ignored the remark and handed the stack of mail to her mother. "Don't forget, we have that new guest coming in this weekend. If he stays as long as he's made reservations for, we'll have to make sure we have everything we need."

Charley frowned and glared at Mom. "And who is that, and how long is he staying?"

Mom grabbed Charley's arm and escorted her down to the lawn and out toward her car. "His name is Clayton Hill, and he's working on some project. Said he wanted a quiet place to work and study for a month or two."

"Is he single or married?" Charley turned back to glance at Jolie.

"I have no idea, and I'm not going to pry." They continued on to Charley's car and out of hearing range for Jolie.

Charley's heart was in the right place, but no amount of matchmaking could be done without a match to make it with, and until more eligible men showed up in Weinberg, Mom and her friends would have little to do in finding a beau for her.

~

Clayton Hill closed his computer and set it aside. He really should start packing, but trying to come up with enough tension and conflict in that last scene had drained him dry. Maybe when he got to Weinberg and the quiet of a small town, he'd be able to concentrate on the troubles for his hero. If he remembered correctly, bluebonnets would be in full bloom, and he loved the sea of blue and purple they created on the landscape. Besides, they might even be an inspiration in his writing.

His cell phone vibrated on the desk beside his laptop, and when his agent's number appeared, he tapped the screen. "Hello, Anne, good news or bad?"

"Both. First, the good news is that when this manuscript is turned in, they're ready for the next series of Jake Reed novels by Clive Hendrix. They've upped the advance for three new ones."

Clay all but shouted. "Yes, that is good news, so what's the bad?"

Her sigh came through the phone. "They can't extend the deadline."

"That's not a problem now. This weekend I'm headed off to a retreat where I can write and get it done in plenty of time. I'll be there until the manuscript is finished…on time."

"Oh, and where are you going?"

"I'm not telling. You have my cell phone number in case you need to reach me. I'm using my real name instead of my pen name. Should have a little more peace and quiet that way."

Anne grumbled with a few words he didn't get, but then her voice turned cheerful. "Well, at least you'll be able to work. I promise not to bother you unless something really important comes up."

"Good. I'll hold you to that. I'm driving up tomorrow, and I'll be there in time to check in for the evening and get settled. They advertised free Wifi, so I'll email you. We can keep in contact that way." The less contact he had with the outside world, the better off he'd be, but his agent would never stand for being cut off completely from him.

"All right, but do send me a few chapters along the way, so I can keep abreast of what you're doing."

"Will do, and thanks for all your effort for me with Anne. I'll be on the look-out for the new contract." He ended the call and headed to the kitchen for a lunch break. After eating, he finished packing and loaded his car.

He gazed around the apartment before closing and locking the door. It was quite enough for the most part, but he had too many distractions with the TV, neighbors, and friends calling at all hours.

"Clayton Hill!"

Clay jumped at the sound and dropped his keys.

Mrs. Sorenson, his next door neighbor tapped his arm. "I'm so sorry, my boy, I didn't mean to startle you."

"It's okay. Now, what can I do for you?"

"I see you're leaving town. Going to be gone long?" She peered up at him with clear blue eyes behind gold rimmed glasses.

"Yes, I am. Working on my new book."

"Oh, I'm so glad." She clapped her hands. "You know I'll keep watch on your apartment for you."

"Thank you, Mrs. Sorenson." Clay hugged her. His eighty year-old neighbor had an eagle eye for things going on around the complex, so he had no worries about being gone for the next two months.

"You have the extra key, and you have my cell phone number, so you can contact me if there's a problem."

She reached up and patted his cheek. "You're such a fine young man. I do hope you'll find yourself a nice girl and fall in love." With a final smile she turned and headed back to her apartment.

He locked up and strolled down to his car. Before turning the ignition, he picked up the brochure from the Bluebonnet Bed and Breakfast Inn. It had only opened last Labor Day, but that meant it'd be fresh and clean, the perfect spot for a two month get-away because he didn't plan to leave there until his manuscript was on its way through cyberspace to his editor.

Mrs. Sorenson's last words rang in his ears. Finding a woman and falling in love ranked last on his list of things to do in the near future.

Chapter 2

*J*olie checked the guest reservation list. Two families had booked for the next weekend, but this Clayton Hill planned to be a guest for up to two months. He would be the first to stay longer than a week, and this fact raised Jolie's curiosity to the max. Why in the world would a man want to stay at a bed and breakfast for that long?

The front door opened with a bang and Charley burst through with Darlene Williams close behind.

"Sorry, Ladies, mom's not here. She's gone to town to pick up a few things."

Charley shook her head. "We're not here to see your mother. We're here to see you. Tell her, Darlene."

Darlene laid a flyer on the counter of the

registration desk. "We need your help with our garden club booth for the fair."

"These are already being circulated around town, and we have some here to give to guests. What do you want me to do with it?" Jolie smoothed out the sheet and frowned.

"Charley and I spoke with the chairman of the fair committee and she said it'd be all right for us to use the logo from this on the banners for our booth. What we need is for you to incorporate it into a design for a banner to display in our booth. You're good with the computer and graphic stuff, so will you do it for us?"

She had nothing better to do on her calendar for the week ahead. "I suppose I could. It's still two weeks off, so I should have time to design something using your logo. Give me all the specifications and I'll get started on it on soon as I can. We do have a business to run here, and our guests come first."

Charley poked her friend. "See, Darlene, I told you she'd do it."

"Thank you, Jolie. We really appreciate your help." She pulled a sheet of paper from her over-sized tote purse. "Here is what we need, and if we can get the design to us by the end of the week, we can get it over to the printers have the banners made. That way we'll have them to put up first thing on Saturday."

Jolie sighed and took the paper. Why did Charley have to be so right all the time? "Okay, I'll try to have something ready for you by Friday. Plenty of time for you to place it on your booth." Her first instinct had been to ask why they didn't just let the sign shop take care of it, but she suspected Mom had something to do with that.

The ladies hit each other's elbows with a satisfied grin and scurried back outside for who knew what. She glanced down at the paper and chuckled. At least what they wanted didn't require a lot of time. Most of the design jobs tackled back in Houston had been much more difficult than this.

She laid the paper aside and checked the breakfast menu for the next week. With the new guest, they would have to add a guest breakfast on Monday mornings. That was the only problem with a long-term guest. Mondays were clean-up and preparations day with the tearoom closed. They'd still do those things, but would now have to keep this Clayton Hill in mind as they performed their chores.

The dryer buzzed from the laundry room in the back of the house to remind her of one aspect of the day needed completion. Making sure all seven guest rooms had clean linens would fill the remainder of the morning. By then, Mom would be back from her grocery shopping and have all the supplies stashed away.

Daisy Martin, a young woman hired on to help with the daily cleaning poked her head through the open office door. "I'm off to put these towels away and finish tidying upstairs."

"Thanks, I'm right behind you to finish the beds." Jolie closed down the computer and headed for the laundry room Mom had added near the back entrance. The mundane chores like changing the linens gave her time to think about ways to improve the inn and the tearoom. With the way the tearoom had taken off, they stayed busy throughout the four days of the week they opened.

If Mom had her way, the tearoom would have been open six days a week, but Jolie had won that argument with help from Bertha, their kitchen helper. Between Mom and Bertha, some of the best food in town was served between eleven in the morning and two in the afternoon, Wednesdays through Saturdays.

About a half hour later a car door slammed outside and Jolie hurried down to help Mom with the groceries. "Glad you're back. Did you get all your errands run?"

"Yes, I did. Beautiful day for it. Will you bring the insulated bags? Want to get those foods into the freezer right away." Mom grabbed a tote bag filled with produce.

Jolie lifted the bags from the back of her mom's van and followed her into the kitchen. "Mr. Hill is due to check in at four. His room's all ready. I hope he likes the suite on the third floor. It should be quieter than the ones over the tearoom."

"I'm sure everything will be fine, dear. With few if any guests during the week and the tearoom open only a few hours a day, Mr. Hill should have all the quiet he wants for his project."

And just what that project might be is what whetted Jolie's curiosity the most.

~

Clay drove into Weinberg and grinned in satisfaction. Just the type of small town atmosphere he needed for inspiration. Trees dotted spaces between sidewalks and streets and many of the business sported striped awnings offering both advertisement for the establishment and shelter from sun.

The majority of the buildings were red brick with trimmings of the native off-white stone found in quarries around the area, a fact he'd picked up in researching one of his earlier novels. The white against red made for a charming contrast.

The lazy, friendly atmosphere already relaxed his muscles, tense from driving the hilly roads off the interstate. He glanced at his GPS to find the Bluebonnet Inn to be several blocks ahead. A banner touting the upcoming Bluebonnet Fair swung across the main street of town, and up ahead the county courthouse lifted its clock tower to the sky.

He checked his watch with the clock tower and chuckled. Right on time to the minute. Somebody took good care of maintenance around here. Since he'd decided to leave his fancy, foreign sports car at home and rent a mid-size sedan, no one paid any attention to him. Just the way he hoped to keep it.

A sign above one of the buildings announced

the *Between the Pages* bookstore. Of course a small town would have a bookstore, but the chances of anyone recognizing him as the author of a best-selling spy espionage series were remote, especially since he planned to use his real name while here.

After two turns, he spotted the big white house trimmed in blue up ahead. The big sign sporting the name of the inn and the flower in its name welcomed him. Another smaller sign indicated guest parking in the rear. He decided to check in first and then park later. The wrap- around porch with its wicker chairs and porch beckoned him to an afternoon of leisure. Maybe he'd spend some time there.

He climbed the steps and crossed the porch to open the door same color as the famed flower. An oval glass window etched in the same design as the sign out front. One thing for sure, they were proud of the flower as well they should be.

An empty foyer greeted him with the reception desk to his left. He rang the old fashioned bell sitting on the counter. A moment later a door behind the desk opened and the loveliest image he'd seen yet stepped out to meet him. Dark blonde hair pulled back in a pony-tail swung as she closed the door and graced him with a dazzling smile and sparkling eyes.

"Hello, and welcome to Bluebonnet Inn. You must be Clayton Hill. I'm Jolie Burns, the owner's daughter." Her smile revealed even, white teeth that must have bought some fine things for an orthodontist years ago.

He stood there speechless until her brow furrowed above eyes the color of the flower decorating everything. "I'm sorry, yes, I'm Clayton Hill."

She placed a registration book in front of him. "If you'll sign in here along with your license plate number, I'll get your room key."

"Um...oh...thank you." He bent over the book and scrawled his name and required number on the page then handed her his credit card. "I'd like to pay by the week if that's suitable."

"Of course, Mr. Hill." After swiping the card, she reached into a cubby-hole and pulled out a key dangling from an oblong antique leather tag that reminded him of his grandfather's watch fob. "You're in room 31 at the head of the stairs on the third floor. It should be a quieter area and looks out over the creek that runs across the back of the property."

When he grasped the key, his fingers wrapped around hers for a moment, and warmth shot up his arm, straight to his heart. She jerked back her hand and pushed the credit slip forward for him to sign.

"Will you be able to get your own luggage? Our boy who handles bags works only on the weekends as that's when we have the most guests."

Clay tightened his fist about the key and signed the receipt. "Not a problem. I don't have that much with me." Now that sounded dumb since he planned to stay two months. He'd been here five minutes and sounded more like the country boy coming to the city than the other way around.

"Fine. You'll notice a sign on the back of your door stating all our policies. If you have any questions and no one is here, just ring the bell. Hope you enjoy your stay."

He stepped back to leave.

"And one other thing, we only provide breakfast every morning to guests. Lunch in the tearoom is extra and we're open for lunch only four days a week. A list of places to eat in town is on the desk in your room."

Clay tipped his fingers in salute and hurried back to his car. One thing he hadn't expected was to find a gorgeous woman hiding away at a bed and breakfast in a small town. She belonged in Dallas or Houston. He opened the back door of the car and pulled out his computer bag before opening the trunk to get his rolling bag. He jerked to a stop with his hand ready to pull out the suitcase. Not here. He had to park in the rear.

He slung the computer bag into the trunk and slammed the lid. How could one woman have such an effect on him in less than ten minutes? That was one distraction he didn't need and he'd better concentrate on business or he'd be in hot water in more ways than one.

Chapter 3

*S*oon as the front door closed behind Clay, Jolie leaned against the desk and let her breath out in whoosh. Nobody had prepared her for the hunk of man Clayton Hill turned out to be. Eyes the color of her favorite dark chocolates and hair only a little lighter sent her heart into a tailspin. Not to mention that even if she wore her highest heels, he'd still be a good three inches or so taller than she was.

Then anxiety reared its ugly head. Charley and the others would have a field day with this. Mr. Hill had to be close to Jolie's age if not older, and that's just the sort of fodder they hunted to plant the seeds of romance. No telling what those ladies would cook up. Her best bet had to be to head them off at the pass. But how?

Jolie plopped onto the chair behind the registration desk. She hadn't seen anyone as handsome as Clayton Hill since she'd left Houston last summer. If she had time to be interested in anyone, he fit the bill, but she didn't have the time or the desire.

Mom stepped into the hall from the kitchen. "I heard a car pulling around to back guest lot. Mr. Hill check in?"

"Yes, he did. He should be bringing his bags inside any minute." She wished the back entrance didn't run past the laundry room and storage facilities and that they had a back stairway.

"Hmm. What's he like? Must be an old hermit if wants complete privacy and quiet to work on some project. You be sure to tell him there won't be much peace and quiet when it comes Bluebonnet Fair time."

The back door opened. "Why don't you tell him yourself? He's on his way in." She stepped around the desk so she could see her mother's face when she met Mr. Hill.

He moved from the door with his back toward them, pulling his huge rolling bag over the threshold. Jolie sensed her mother stiffening beside her. Clayton Hill's back and shoulders were most definitely not those of a hermit or recluse.

She hid her grin when he turned and stopped.

He stopped in front of them with a sheepish grin and a nod toward her mother. "Good afternoon, Ma'am. I'm your new guest."

Mom's quick intake of breath and gaping mouth were what Jolie expected. She hadn't been prepared to meet this gorgeous man either.

Her mother recovered and offered her hand to Mr. Hill. "Welcome to Bluebonnet Inn, Mr. Hill. I'm Emma Sue Burns, the owner and manager." She stepped back to allow him to pass.

"Good to meet you, Mrs. Burns." He nodded to them both and continued on his way.

Her mother's eyes opened wide and she fanned her face with her fingers. Her mouth formed one silent word. "Wow."

Jolie chuckled. When he stopped at the bottom of the stairway and looked back at them, she squelched it and straightened her posture.

"I see you have one of those chair lift things. Nice for your disabled guests." He grinned at them then tromped up the stairs to his room.

"Jolie! You could have warned me. He's not at all what I expected. She flung the dishtowel she'd been holding to land on her shoulder. "Wait until I tell the girls about this."

Jolie groaned. The race had begun, and she may as well give Mr. Hill fair warning. He wouldn't know what had hit him when those ladies stirred up a plot and took him on as their project. He may be here to work on his own, but now he'd become the subject of one far greater than any he could ever concoct.

She sat down at the desk and rested her forehead on her hands. The one thing she dreaded most was the way the ladies would be so cutesy but obvious in their ploys to get her involved with Mr. Hill. One part of her might gladly participate while another part of her bemoaned the fact of how unfair it was to Mr. Hill. She'd just have to meet with him later this evening and tell him what to expect.

"Jolie, come help me in the kitchen."

"Coming, Mom." She headed toward her mother's voice and walked in as her mother laid her phone on the counter. "Just finished a group text to the girls. They'll all be here for breakfast in the morning to meet our Mr. Hill for themselves."

"Mom! That's terrible. Our guests expect to eat their meal in peace and not be gawked at by a bunch of old women."

Her mother tilted her head and swung one fist up to her hip. "For goodness sakes, honey. They won't be gawking. They'll come in for breakfast like they sometimes do and that's that. Besides, we're not as old as you think. We can still appreciate a good-looking man."

If it were only that, Jolie wouldn't mind so much, but when Charley, Darlene, Ava Lou, and Ellen got together with a scheme or a plan, the rest of the world better watch out.

~

Clay laid his laptop on the desk then hoisted his suitcase to the carrier provided. He rubbed his hands together and surveyed the room. Very nice for a small town. Although not as large as a hotel room suite, it had everything he needed, from the queen size bed, to the navy blue upholstered lounge chair and oversized desk in the sitting area that led to a balcony overlooking the front lawn.

Navy blue and cream decorated the room with the comforter on the bed matching the curtains on the windows and the lamp shades. Definitely a unisex room. No extra frills, but two vases of fresh flowers provided just the right touch without being too feminine.

He unzipped his suitcase and lifted out the zipper bag with all his underwear rolled inside. He'd learned that trick from his mother and it had served him well in all his travels the past few years. An antique style armoire held four deep drawers for belongings on one side and a mirror on the other. After stashing the essentials, he reached for his shaving kit and headed for the bathroom.

Here navy blue towels hung on chrome racks against walls painted the same cream color as the bedroom. A sink sat in the middle of large cabinet that gave him ample space for all his grooming gear. Behind a navy blue shower curtain he found a bathtub which gave him the option of a shower or a bath.

So far everything checked out to be as nice as the brochure had described. The two women he'd met downstairs had done an excellent job if the other rooms were as welcoming as this. The beautiful old Victorian style home held just the right amount of charm to be comfortable and a place he could work in peace.

Remembering what Miss Burns had said, he strode over to the door to find the list of "House Rules." Her face with its well-defined cheek bones kept interfering with the words on the framed list. Most were standard hotel rules, including the hours for breakfast and the tearoom, but a couple of them brought a chuckle. Number ten stated that no un-registered guests of the opposite sex were allowed upstairs in the bedroom area. All guests were to be entertained in the downstairs parlor. Number eleven stated that the TV in each room must be turned off by midnight each night to avoid disturbing the other guests.

He'd have no problem with those two rules, but the next one puzzled him. It stated the refrigerator held items that were free, and he could add his own as he liked, and the microwave and coffeepot should be cleaned after use.

A refrigerator, microwave and coffeepot? He glanced around the room. He saw no evidence of any of them anywhere. Then it hit him. Of course...the armoire. He hadn't noticed the small handle on the mirror before, but when he pulled it, the mirror opened, and there sat the listed items. After closing the mirror and then the doors, he sauntered over to the back windows. Miss Burns and her mother knew how to make their guests feel at home. Not only was she beautiful, but Miss Burns appeared to be a smart business woman as well.

The view from the one large window provided a picture of stately oaks and elms, but also glimpses of the hills beyond, and the creek Miss Burns had mentioned. Nice for gazing and thinking.

Figures in the parking lot drew his attention. Miss Burns stood with two women who gestured wildly and pointed to his room. He stepped back and shook his head. Had someone found out who he was? Then he laughed. Those two elderly women were not the type of readers who enjoyed his books. Must be something else going on.

After changing into jeans and knit turtleneck shirt, he grabbed up the restaurant list and headed back downstairs. Maybe Mrs. Burns or her daughter might have a suggestion. A brief thought of asking Miss Burns to join him crossed his mind but he squelched it. That would not be the best way to begin two months of solitude for his writing.

~

"No, Ava Lou, you can't come in and browse and lounge around hoping for some glimpse of Mr. Hill. He's a guest and we assure our guests of their privacy."

"But Darlene said she spotted him downtown in a rental car, and she said he's the handsomest man she's ever seen except for her Ben of course."

"Charley, I don't care if she said he's the man on the moon; you two are not going to pester him before he even gets settled."

"But we just want to see him...er...I mean meet him."

"I know what you meant, Ava Lou, and it's not gonna happen. Maybe you'll see him if you stop by the tearoom for lunch one day this week."

Charley's grin grew wide as the outdoors. "Or maybe we can stop in for breakfast tomorrow. After all, your mother did invite us."

Jolie groaned and shook her head. "Okay, okay. See him at breakfast tomorrow, but go on home now and leave the poor man alone for one night."

"Guess that'll have to do for now. C'mon, Ava Lou, let's go see Darlene and Ellen. We gotta coordinate our timing for tomorrow morning." She pivoted on the balls of her feet and strode to her car.

The two ladies climbed back into Charley's Buick and waved good-bye. Jolie shook her head again. The next two months were going to be very interesting to say the least.

Chapter 4

*J*olie hurried back to the house to talk with her mother about the behavior of her friends. When she reached the front desk, Mr. Hill stepped down from the stairway.

"Oh, hello, Mr. Hill, I trust you found your room to your liking."

"Yes, it's exactly what I need for my project. I really didn't expect a suite like that."

"We decided to reserve the third floor room for longer term guests, and you're our first one." Heat rose up her neck with that last statement. Now he'd think they didn't run a good business. "What I mean is usually our guests are here only for the week-ends or for a few days. We weren't sure we'd need the suite, but now I'm glad we have it available for you, Mr. Hill."

"Please call me Clay. Mr. Hill makes me feel old."

His grin revealed crinkles fanning from his eyes which added to his charm. "All right, I will do that, and I'm Jolie. No sense in formalities since you're going to be around a while."

"I see you're headed out to find a meal in our fair town." She gestured toward the menu list in his hand.

"No, he isn't." Mom strode down the hall, a determined smile gracing her lips. "You're going to have dinner with us, Mr. Hill. There's plenty of what I've prepared."

Jolie pressed her lips together. Mom never cooked more than the two of them could eat. She'd planned this as soon as he'd appeared this afternoon.

"That's very nice of you, Mrs. Burns, but I don't want to impose my first night here."

Mom swung her dishtowel over her shoulder, a gesture meaning her mind was made up. "No imposition at all. It'll be nice to have company." She stared at Jolie. "Won't it, honey?"

"Yes, it will." No sense in disagreeing at this point. Besides, it would be nice to have a a third at the table, especially one as good looking as Clay.

"Then it's all settled. We'll eat in the nook off the kitchen. That's where Jolie and I usually eat." She spun on her toes and gestured for Clay to follow her.

He grinned, tipped his fingers in salute, and

followed Mom.

Jolie shook her head. Mom would be up to her old tricks and would know Clayton Hill's complete life history before dessert.

The table had room for six, but only three places at one end were set. The aroma of Jolie's favorite King Ranch Chicken casserole permeated the air and Jolie's stomach rumbled. She sat down on one side of the table with Clay on the other side. That left the place at the end for her mother.

A salad and a bowl of guacamole sat in the near the middle of the table as well as a bowl of salsa. Mom brought in the casserole and set it on the trivet in the center. "I'll be back with the warm tortillas in a sec. Go ahead and sit, Clay."

In a moment she returned with both the warm soft tortillas and a bowl of crisp tortilla chips. "Jolie and I usually drink water with our meals, but if you'd like sweet tea, I can make it real quick."

"No, no thank you. Water is fine."

Mom took her chair. "Well, then, let's have our prayer and we can eat." She stretched out both hands. Clay's brow furrowed a moment before he grasped her left hand. "We thank You for Your bounty, oh Lord. We thank you for our guest, Clayton Hill. May he find what he needs for his project. Bless this food now to our use and bless us to Your service. Amen."

"Help yourself, young man. There's plenty here." Mom handed Clay the serving spoon.

Indeed, there was. Mom had never made a

casserole this big for just the two them. It was one of the tearoom specials and everyone raved about it. Looked like she'd be having casserole for the next few days.

"Now tell me, Clayton, what do you do in Dallas? Unusual for a man to be able to take off for two months. Do you own your own business?"

The startled look in Clay's eyes matched the panic on his face. She should have taken time to warn him that her mother wanted to everything about her guests. However, Jolie was just as interested in his answer as her mother.

His face took on a more relaxed expression, and he smiled. "Yes, I do have my own business, but it's not the usual kind of business. I work by contract for others and take care of whatever needs to be done. I didn't have any new jobs right away thus the ability to get time away."

As vague as that answer was to Jolie, it seemed to satisfy Mom because she went right on with more questions about his life, not his job. However, Jolie's curiosity about his so-called *project* intrigued her.

"Do you have family in Dallas, Clayton, or did you move away from them like Jolie did us when she graduated college?"

"Mother, that's none of your business. I'm sorry, Clay. Mom sometimes gets carried away."

"It's okay, Jolie. Yes, I did move to Dallas after graduation from OU. My family lives in Oklahoma. You go where the job opportunities are after college. Right, Jolie."

Jolie jerked her head back and blinked. "Hm, yes, I suppose you do."

"And where did you go to college, and how did you wind up back here?"

Neat trick, Mr. Hill. Turn attention away from yourself and onto others. She almost laughed. He had no idea how persistent her mother could be about gleaning information from single young men.

"I graduated from Baylor and went to Houston as a graphic arts specialist and worked for a company designing websites and whatever else came my way."

"Oh, so you're computer savvy."

"I suppose you could say I am. That's one reason I came home. After Dad died and my three brothers were busy with their own families, this house was too large for Mom to take care of so she turned it into a bed and breakfast. My sisters-in-law took care of the decorating and I took care of all the publicity and promotion."

"Looks like you've done an excellent job with it, Mrs. Burns."

"Thank you, Clayton. We had a few setbacks, but we managed to open on time. You must be single too, or did you leave family in Dallas?"

Heat filled Jolie's face and she bent her head over her food to hide the fact she blushed yet again. Would her mother never give up?

"As a matter of fact I am single. No ties that bind anywhere." He wink and grinned at Jolie.

At least he seemed to know what he was up against. She relaxed her shoulders and her cheeks cooled.

"Well now, isn't that nice." Mom pushed back her chair. "Time for dessert. I hope you like Lemon Meringue Pie. It's one the favorites in our tearoom."

After dessert, Mom left Jolie with Clayton. No kitchen duty for Jolie tonight. She crushed her napkin and laid it on the table. Now what was she supposed to do? Mom was up to her old tricks. Jolie sighed and rose from the table. "I'm so sorry, Clay. Mom can really be nosy sometimes.

~

Clay followed Jolie into a sitting area off the main entrance. She sat on one of the upholstered chairs near the fireplace. When he sat opposite her, he spotted what looked like the tearoom through the French doors behind her.

"I understand her wanting to know about her guests, especially when one will be staying as long as I am."

She said nothing but settled back into her chair and crossed her legs.

He gestured toward the room behind the doors. "Is that the tearoom where your guests usually eat breakfast?"

"Yes, and it's also open to the public every morning except Mondays and Sundays. Only guests are served then." She bit her bottom lip and frowned.

Something must be troubling her, but he wouldn't be nosy and ask what it might be. While he hadn't told the entire truth at the dinner table, he hadn't lied when he said he had no new jobs right away, and it would stay that way if he didn't get this present contract fulfilled.

Jolie uncrossed her legs and leaned forward, her hands on her knees. "Clay, I have to be honest with you and warn you about a few things that will most likely happen in the next few days."

"And what would I need warning about in a town as nice as Weinberg?" The only fear he had was of recognition, and that wasn't likely to happen in this small town.

"Hmm, well you see, Mom has these friends. They have some silly notion that I should at least have a boyfriend since I'm not married. They've tried to hitch me up with every single male who comes into town, and you won't be the exception."

"They can't be all that bad. Clay chuckled and shook his head. "Although I'm sure it isn't pleasant for you."

Red flushed her face, and Jolie bit her lip again. "Let's see what you think after they begin their little schemes and plots to get us two together."

This time he had to laugh out loud. "Oh, Jolie, don't let it get to you. All my friends in Dallas try to do the same thing with me. Can't tell you how many blind dates I've had in the last several months."

A smile turned up the corners of her mouth. "I

guess if you're single, every married or once married person thinks you should be married, too. They don't have much to work with in this small town, so you're prime fodder for their schemes."

"You're right about that." He settled back and tapped his fingertips together. "Give me some idea of what they're like and who they are."

"Well, if I'm correct, you'll meet them for breakfast in the morning. Two of them have already been here asking about you, and said they'd be here tomorrow bright and early."

"Oh, that must have been the two women I saw you talking with in the parking lot earlier."

Jolie groaned. "You saw them. They were trying to get into the house and find you right then, but I headed them off at the pass so to speak. You see what we're up against?"

"Tell me more. You really have my curiosity aroused." He couldn't imagine what trouble a few women could cause, but it might be interesting to find out.

"You asked for it. First, there's mother's best friend, Charlie, short for Charlene. She's a widow with a mind of her own and doesn't mind sharing her opinions with everyone in sight. She has a heart as good as gold and as big as all get out, but it isn't always in sync with her motives."

"Sounds like my aunt Mildred. Go on. How many are there."

She swallowed hard before answering. "Five, including Mom."

Five? He'd considered three, but five would be a lot to handle. "That's a crowd, not a group."

"I'm glad to see you can smile about it. We'll see if it's still there when I'm finished."

She tucked her feet under her legs and leaned on the chair arm. "Next is Darlene. She's married to the contractor who did the remodeling work on the house. Then Ava Lou owns the beauty shop and she's married to a lawyer. Last, but not least, is Ellen Benton, the owner of our bookstore."

At the last name, Clay gulped. The book storeowner was friends with Mrs. Burns? That put a whole new light on the situation as well as the plan that had been forming in his head. "Sounds like quite a bunch of ladies."

"They are and like I said, you'll meet them in the morning."

The plan he'd been thinking might not work now, but it would have to do. Anything that would help the ladies at their game and leave him alone had to work. "Jolie, I have an idea. At first, it may sound crazy, but hear me out."

She raised her eyebrows. "Okay. So what's your idea?"

"Let's beat the ladies at their own game. You say they're always cooking up ways to get you a date, so let's go along with them. After the second trick or so, we can act like we really hit it off and plan to see a lot of each other. That way I can get my work done, and they won't be harassing you."

"That does sound crazy, but knowing Mom's

friends, it just might put them off track. But if you have to work, how are going to keep up appearances of dating?"

"We both have to eat, so we can dine out at different places, and maybe I can spare one evening or so for a movie. If I work all day or at least most of the day, a few evenings won't hurt."

Jolie scrunched her nose then burst out laughing. "It's so wild, but it may be just the thing to throw Mom's friends into a tailspin."

"So are you in?"

"You bet I am. I've always wanted to see them get taken down a peg or two."

Now that it was settled, Clay could count on a little more privacy to get his book finished. No way would he let a few busy-body ladies spoil his work time. He had a deadline to meet. Besides, being with Jolie would be fun. The one thing he had to remember was that it was only a game of pretend, not real and only for two months.

Chapter 5

At five the next morning, Jolie helped her mother and Bertha prepare breakfast for the inn. The tearoom opened at six-thirty, so they had plenty of time to have the buffet ready to go. Bertha rolled out her biscuits and Mom cracked eggs into a large stainless steel bowl. Jolie's job was to fry bacon. Grits, muffins, and assorted sweet rolls rounded out Tuesday's menu. Fruit had been prepared and was ready to serve as well.

Jerry Anderson opened the back door and stepped inside with arms loaded. "Good morning, Mrs. Burns. Here's your bakery order. Cream cheese and fruit kolaches are included this morning along with the muffins."

"Thanks, Jerry. Set the boxes on the counter. Jolie, will you get the money for him?"

"Sure." Jolie strode to the office and wrote out the check. Anderson's Bakery had been supplying their breads for breakfast and the tearoom lunches and they were a big hit. Saved time for Mom and Bertha in the kitchen as well.

She returned with the check and handed it to Jerry. "Here's the order for the rest of the week as well. Your mom said she had a new whole grain bread recipe, so I added a couple of loaves of that to the usual. I noticed she had some new nut breads as well, so I added different ones for variety."

"Oh, you'll love the new breads. Mom made us a loaf of the whole grain for Sunday dinner, and it's delicious. Makes great sandwiches, too. See ya' tomorrow."

After he left, the kitchen filled with the aromas of frying meat, baking biscuits and eggs. Promptly at six-thirty, Jolie left to open the tearoom for breakfast. She unlocked the door and spotted three of her mother's friends driving around to the side to park.

The bottom stair squeaked, and she turned to find Clay bouncing on it. "Reminds me of home. Our stairway had one squeaky stair, and I always stepped over it when I got in later than usual."

"Yeah, I've done the same with that one a time or two in the past."

The door burst open and the three women breezed in with Charley in the lead. She came to a dead-stop of the sight of Clay in the entryway. "Oh, my. You're up early."

Ava Lou and Darlene stared from behind Charley.

Jolie laughed and shook her head. Ellie must have decided not to join them. "Good morning, ladies. Meet Clayton Hill, our latest guest."

Oozing charm from every pore, Clay stepped forward with a slight bow. "I'm so pleased to meet friends of Mrs. Burns. She's told me about you, and that you would be here for breakfast. If the aroma tells me right, we're in for quite a treat for our meal."

The ladies stared, open mouthed and wide-eyed.

Clay chuckled, stepped to the side and waved his arm toward the tearoom. "Shall we see what's on the buffet, ladies?"

The ladies became a mass of swinging arms and pocketbooks in an attempt to be first in line. Jolie swallowed hard and pressed her lips together to keep from bursting out in laughter. Oh, he was going to play this to the hilt. These women wouldn't know what hit them before it was all over. The week ahead looked a whole lot brighter than it had yesterday at this time.

Other regular breakfast customers came in and greeted Jolie before heading for the tearoom and the buffet. Daisy came in the back way and apologized for being late.

"I'm so sorry, Jolie. I just couldn't get going this morning." She peeked around the corner to the tearoom. "Oh my, looks like a few more than the regulars are here this morning. I best be getting my apron and getting to work. I'm glad to see Maxine is already here."

"You're fine, Daisy. Most of them just now went in to be seated. I'll get them started with the coffee."

A few minutes later, both she and Daisy served coffee and water to those who had arrived and taken advantage of the buffet while Maxine took care of replenishing the food. Charley, Darlene, and Ava Lou chose a table that left one between them and Clay. The three chattered like magpies, all the while shooting glances his way.

Clay smiled at them then went back to his tablet where Jolie had glimpsed a newspaper website. Jolie had to admit he was one cool gentleman, and the ladies were drowning in his charm.

When he was ready to leave, he gathered up his tablet and phone. He stopped at the ladies' table on his way out. "It was a pleasure to meet you. I'm sure I'll see more of you in the next two months." With a smile, he tapped his forehead with two fingers and left them gawking like birds on a wire.

Oh, he was going all out to impress them this morning. Too bad Ellen couldn't have been here as well. No doubt she'd know all the details before time for morning break since Charley would most certainly make a dash to the bookstore as soon as she left the tearoom.

Jolie sauntered by their table. Once again they argued about who was going to pay. Why they didn't each pay their own bill mystified Jolie even after her mother told her the ladies liked to treat each other.

She stopped at the ladies' table. "I hate to interrupt, but I wondered what you thought of our guest."

Charley stretched and rolled her shoulders. "He seemed nice enough."

"Handsome as all get out, you mean." Darlene rolled her eyes and hugged her hands to her heart.

"Now there's a man I could fall for if I were thir…er…a few years younger." Ava Lou added her two cents.

Charley pushed back on her chair waving the ticket and a few bills in her hand. "Let's go, ladies. We have places to go and people to see."

The other two scrambled for their handbags and trailed after Charley.

If Jolie had to guess, and she didn't, the ladies would head straight to the bookstore and fill in Ellie with all the details of this morning.

Chapter 6

*E*xactly as Jolie had suspected, on Tuesday evening, Mom went to great lengths to make sure Clay knew about and would attend the pot-luck supper at the church. After breakfast on Wednesday morning, Jolie stopped him at the foot of the stairway before he headed to his room.

"Clay, you really don't have to go along with this. Mom gave the excuse that she's going early to help in the kitchen, so you could come in your own car later. You see their plan, don't you?"

"Oh, yes. They'll find some excuse to leave the church early or have something else to do and ask me to bring you back here."

He really did know how their minds worked. Still, she didn't want him to feel obligated to go along with everything they cooked up. "And you don't mind that?"

His deep, rich voice enhanced his laughter. "Of course I don't. We can pretend it's a bother and we don't want to do it, but then we will and make them think they're putting us together."

Jolie clasped her hands to her chest and giggled. "You really are something, Clay Hill."

"Thank you, I think. Anyway, the sooner we can get them out of their plotting and in to thinking they've succeeded, the more privacy I can have, and the more work I can get done. Now I'm off to do some of that work now. See you at lunch." He bounded up the steps, around the corner and out of sight.

Jolie collapsed into the chair behind the registration desk. He really did see this as only a way to get the ladies out of his hair. That most likely meant he wanted to be rid of her as well.

Jolie shook her shoulders. She didn't have time to bother with men now, so why was she even concerned with the idea? Maybe it was a blow to her self-esteem. After all, she wasn't that hard on the eyes. One thing for sure, if he wanted to treat this as a real game, she'd do exactly the same...no matter how much charm went straight to her heart.

Jolie cleared her head of Clay Hill and strolled back to the kitchen. Time to get to work on lunch. The tearoom would open at eleven as usual for a Wednesday morning. Her assignment was to put prepare the fruits for the salads and to slice the oranges to have them ready to adorn the plates when other salads were ordered.

Without saying anything to her mother, Jolie opened the refrigerator and took out the fresh fruits purchased yesterday afternoon. She'd leave the apples and bananas whole, but the berries needed to be washed and the pineapple sliced.

Her mother wrapped her arm about Jolie's waist. "Honey, I hope you don't mind my asking Clay to join us at the pot-luck. He does have to eat, and he'll find no better food than what the ladies of our church can provide."

"I don't mind, but I wouldn't want him to feel obligated to attend."

Both her mother and Bertha looked like kittens lapping cream. Her mother said, "It sure didn't look like he felt obligated to do anything. In fact, I think he looked rather pleased to be invited."

Jolie cringed. If Mom only knew what was going on, she might not be so chipper. "At least he does know his way to the church since you've assigned us to early duty."

"Oh, posh, you don't have to come early with me." Mom waved her hand in the air. "You can stay here and come later with Clay. That would give you two a chance to talk and get to know each other." With that she kissed Jolie's cheek and disappeared into the pantry.

Nothing subtle about her mother. She certainly had wasted no time in getting the ball rolling. No telling what else would happen after tonight. She grinned and sliced into the pineapple. The ladies at church who hadn't yet met Clay would be falling all over themselves to do so, especially if Charley and the others had spread the word about how handsome and charming he was. Let them think all they wanted. To her he was simply a guest who planned to stay a longer time than usual. She'd had enough of city men and their ways.

~

After Clay learned Jolie would be riding with him to the church supper, he took extra care with his clothing. Because the evenings were still chilly, he chose a dark green flannel shirt and khaki slacks to appear casual, but not careless.

He'd been able to get a great deal accomplished today with three new chapters finished and a fourth one was well under way. The only interruption had been lunch in the tearoom. Jolie had been busy with taking care of diners, so he'd returned to his room right away. Maybe they'd have a chance to visit more this evening. Not much though, it couldn't be more than five or six minutes to the church.

Since he still had a half hour before he was to meet Jolie, he opened his laptop to read his email, which he ignored when he was writing. Two were from his agent. One lamented the fact that she didn't know where he was staying and the second asked him to send copies of what he'd written so she could see his progress.

Too bad about the first one. He still didn't plan

to tell her where he was hiding out, but the second one he'd take care of in the morning.

Another message from his sister begged him to come for a visit as soon as he finished this book. His niece and nephew had been asking about their uncle Clay and when he'd come to see them.

He made a note on his calendar to call her to make plans for later in the spring. He loved Tulsa in the springtime and that would be a good time for a visit.

Finally, he could close his computer and head down to the foyer. Why did he look forward to this time with Jolie? He was supposed to be concentrating on his book, not a good-looking woman.

Jolie had her back to him, talking on the phone, when he descended to the first floor. Tonight her hair hung loose and free on her shoulders with just enough wave to tempt his fingers to curl into them. He balled his fists at his sides. He had to get a grip before he lost all thoughts about what he needed to accomplish.

She hung up and swung around to greet him. "Hi, are you ready to go?"

More than ready. "Bring on the ladies and the food. I'll conquer both." He held out his arm for her to grasp.

She clasped her hand around his forearm and grabbed the jacket lying on the desk. "Lead the way then"

When he opened the door for her to slide into

the car, she glanced up at him and grinned. "You're in a good mood. I hope it stays good after Charley, Ava Lou and Darlene are through with you. Ellie will be there as well. You haven't met her yet. You'd already left the tearoom when she arrived at lunch. Should have seen the look on her face when she realized she'd missed—I'm sorry. I'm rambling on like the roses on the back trellis." She ducked her head and pulled in her long, slim legs.

He gulped but leaned down before closing the door. "I'm counting on that ramblin' to tell me more." About what, she'd find out later.

After pulling onto the main street, he asked. "Where did you get a name like Jolie? Don't think I've heard it before."

Her chuckle was barely audible, but it indicated her sense of humor. "It's short for Jolene. My brothers gave it to me when they started leaving off the *n* sound and left the *e*. I added the *ie* so people wouldn't call me Jol."

"Oh, so you have brothers. I have a sister who lives in Tulsa. I hope to go visit her when I'm done here."

"I have three brothers, all married, with seven children among them and another on the way. That's why Mom is so anxious to see me married. She wants more grandchildren."

"My mom's the same way. Sara has two children and Mom is constantly talking about my giving her grandchildren." His palms dampened the steering wheel. Why were they talking about grandchildren? He was nowhere near wanting to talk about family, but he did want to know more about her.

All too soon he pulled into the church parking lot. Maybe he'd learn more on the ride home. He opened the car door and helped her from the front seat. "Guess it's time to face the music, so to speak."

"Yep, and they'll be falling all over themselves to meet you properly." She tilted her head and grinned up at him, her blue eyes dancing with amusement. "I think you can handle them."

But could he handle her? This was not going the way he planned at all. When they entered the fellowship center, he spotted Mrs. Burns with her friends at the serving table. All conversation stopped and all eyes locked on him.

Swallowing hard, Clay approached the ladies. May as well get this over with. "Looks like you have a wonderful selection here. I appreciate your inviting me." He grabbed Jolie's hand and headed for the end of the line.

Jolie giggled and raised their clasped hands between them. "Now this should draw a few comments from the ladies."

Clay grinned. "More fodder for the gossip mill." He held her hand until they reached the end of the serving table and the plates. Every woman behind the table wore a wide grin and greeted him.

"You better try that one." Charley pointed to a casserole dish. "Ava Lou made it and it's delicious."

The dish to which she pointed gave him no clue as to its content, but he wasn't one to disappoint the cook. A spoonful on his plate revealed rice and chicken and something green, possibly broccoli. Nothing wrong with those. "Thank you, Mrs. Sanders and Mrs. Kirk. I'm sure it's good."

Ava Lou Kirk flushed red and shoved Charley with her elbow. "Now don't go so formal on us, young man. Call us by our names. That Mrs. business makes us sound too old."

Behind him Jolie snickered and punched him in the back. This evening might be more fun than he ever thought it could be. When he reached the end of the line, Mrs. Burns called his name.

"Clay, I've saved seats for you over here." She waved a napkin in the air to make sure he and everyone else didn't miss seeing her.

Jolie picked up a glass of tea. "What did I tell you? We'll be together the whole evening."

He lifted his glass of tea to let Mrs. Burns know he saw her. "Isn't that what this whole thing is about anyway? Now let's go have some fun."

Once they were seated, Mrs. Burns introduced him to those sitting nearby. A Mrs. Sikorski pumped his hand. "Sure is good to have a handsome young man staying at our inn. Hope you'll come back and visit us at church."

"I'm sure I will sometime in the next two months." He extracted his hand and picked up a fork but hesitated before taking a bite.

Jolie whispered, "They've said the blessing so go ahead and eat."

How had she known why he hesitated? Getting to know her better was turning out to be quite interesting. He'd have to be a little more careful. He glanced up and spotted Charley, Ava, and Ellie Benton in deep conversation. Ellie must be saying something about him because the other two ladies chose that moment to turn and stare in his direction. When he smiled and acknowledged them, they snapped their heads back around to Ellie.

The bite he'd swallowed soured in his stomach. He sensed they were talking about more than matching him up with Jolie. What if Ellie recognized him? If she had any of his books in her store, she might compare him in person with the man on the back cover. A trip to the bookstore joined his list of things he needed to do in the next few days. If his books were there, he'd have to be a lot more careful than he'd planned. He didn't have the time to be a celebrity.

Chapter 7

*J*olene concentrated on the design on her computer screen. The ladies didn't need it until next week, but she welcomed anything that would get her mind off Clay Hill. She'd enjoyed being with him far more than she'd expected, and it appeared he enjoyed the pot-luck supper. Then on the way home he'd been pre-occupied with something and hardly said half a dozen words to her.

She clicked on the print button and sat back to wait for the machine to spew out her design. Everything about last night had been unusual. Of course the ladies' reaction to his being there had been expected, but several times Clay's eyes had clouded over as though he was thinking something over, and twice he'd eyed the ladies with a wary expression.

What if he regretted the plan to go along with their schemes? It had been his idea, so all he had to do was say he didn't want to go through with it. He'd even taken his breakfast back up to his room this morning rather than eat in the dining room.

"Jolene, has Clayton come back down from his room?'" Mom plopped down in the chair by the desk.

"No, or at least I haven't seen him. I've been busy with the design for the signs for the garden club booth." He could've easily come down the stairs and gone out the back way without her ever seeing him.

"Hmm, I thought it strange that he didn't stay down here for breakfast. The girls were really disappointed." She leaned on the desk with her forearm and peered at Jolie. "Did you have an argument or a disagreement or something last night?"

"No, we didn't. He didn't talk much at all on the way home. I think he was preoccupied with something. I imagine it has to do with his project. Maybe he's behind on it and needs to work extra." Jolie shook herself. Why was she making excuses for a man she'd only known for three days? What he did was none of her business. He was a guest and that was all.

"Ellie said she wanted to talk with him some more because he looked so familiar. She thinks maybe she knows him from somewhere." Mom twisted her mouth in that way she had when the gears in her head started grinding.

"Well, he's from Dallas now, but he's originally from Oklahoma. If she's ever been to either of those places, she may have seen or met him, but I doubt it." Indeed, that was all but impossible as Ellie never traveled anywhere except to a big bookseller's conference every summer.

Mom pushed herself from the chair. "Well, she can see him some other time. I'm going out to the kitchen to help Bertha get ready for the tearoom lunch crowd."

"I'll be in soon as I finish a few orders for supplies."

After retrieving the printout, Jolie closed the program and worked on the supply order. Fresh produce they purchased from the stores here in town, but for others like staples, laundry and cleaning supplies, she ordered in bulk.

Daisy stepped off the stairway with cleaning supplies in hand. "All the rooms are ready for the arrival of guests this weekend. Mr. Hill is still in his room. I don't know when he'll leave so I can clean the bathroom and change the linens."

"Don't worry about it now. If he leaves before the tearoom opens, you can do it then. Otherwise he might have to wait another day." Indeed, if the hours Clay had been keeping since his arrival on Monday were any indication, there would be no set time for cleaning his room.

Daisy nodded and headed to the storage closet to stow her cleaning supplies. The way Clay kept to himself while at the inn sent Jolie's imagination on wild trips to figure out what his "project" might be. She'd never heard of a project where a man holed himself away in a small town and stayed in his room most of the time.

She closed her computer. What he did with his work time was absolutely none of her business. On the way to the kitchen, she stopped at the registration desk and checked the guest reservations for the week-end. One couple was scheduled along with two family groups. She'd make sure the families were on the second floor in the back. They had one room with a connecting bath for especially for ones with younger children. The others had their own private bathrooms. Maybe they wouldn't disturb him as much there.

After a few minutes, she sat down and leaned back to close her eyes. When Clay did venture from his room, he was friendly, and oh so handsome. She almost wished their times together were not part of a game, but he'd be gone in two months, and she'd be back where she had started. Still, it wouldn't hurt to enjoy any time she had with him until he left.

"My, my, you must be thinking of something pleasant."

Jolie's eye lids popped open at Clay's voice and she all but fell from her chair. Heat filled her face as she straightened and pushed her hair back from her face. "I didn't hear you come down the stairs."

"I could tell. You were on another planet." His

deep voice laughed again.

She dropped her gaze to the ledger book to avoid connecting with his. "Do you need anything?"

"No. I'm going out for a while. I'll be gone an hour or so, so you can let Daisy know she can clean up while I'm gone. I'll be back here for lunch, but if I may, I'd like to take it up to my room."

"That's perfectly fine. In fact, you can leave your order, and I'll bring it up to you."

"No, no need for that. I'll take care of it." He started to leave, but stopped and asked, "What time does the bookstore open? I saw the owner here at breakfast."

"Oh, Thursdays are her late days, so she always meets her friends for breakfast here on that day. She opens at ten and stays open until eight tonight."

"Oh, that explains it." A broad grin brought out a twinkle in his eye. "I enjoyed the dinner last night. I think we have them very pleased that their so called scheme to get us together last night worked."

"They sure had enough questions for me this morning. I'm glad we went."

"I am, too. I also enjoyed our time together, and I look forward to doing more things if all works out as they plan."

The mischief in his eyes sent Jolie's heart to fluttering. He did want to spend more time with her even if it was all part of a joke on the ladies.

That didn't matter. She'd take whatever hours she could in the coming weeks. "So do I, and it'll be interesting to see what they cook up next."

This time he did leave, but Jolie sat at the desk staring at the door after he closed it behind him. Never had a man affected her this way in so short a time. Three days and she was as smitten as a school girl with her first crush. She had to remember it was a game and would be over when he left, but she planned to have fun while it lasted.

~

Clay bounded down the steps from the inn then slapped his forehead. Now he had to walk around to the back parking lot for his car. Why hadn't he gone on out the back door to the lot? So much easier. Jolie, that's why. Soon as he'd seen her sitting there with eyes closed and a contented smile on her face, he had to speak to her.

Such a distraction from what he'd intended to do. He jangled his keys in his hand and wished he hadn't been so silent on the way home from the church. His mind had become preoccupied with the whispers and glances from the bookstore owner that he'd let a perfectly good opportunity to get to know Jolie even better slip away.

Then he grinned and clicked the remote to unlock his car. Mrs. Burns and her friends would give him another opportunity for that. What would their next plan be? He chuckled and turned the ignition. Whatever, he planned to enjoy it.

Before he left the lot, he rolled down the

windows to let in the fresh air. Texas had few true spring days to enjoy the moderate temperatures and sunshine, and he wanted to take full advantage on this day. A light breeze stirred the leaves and wafted the scent of Mrs. Burns' roses on the air. He stared at the gazebo. Maybe he and Jolie would have another time to sit out there and talk.

He shrugged and turned the key in the ignition. Better get those thoughts out of his head. He'd come here to work and not spend time with a woman, no matter how pretty she may be. Besides, he'd be leaving in two months, and it wouldn't be fair to her to monopolize her time when nothing could come of a relationship.

Clay drove down the driveway and onto the street. At ten in the morning, people already strolled the streets and browsed in the myriad shops along the way. Weinberg was an old town and the main street shops attracted tourists from all over the state. The sign for the *Between the Pages* bookshop loomed ahead between a gift shop and an antique store.

He spotted an empty space a few doors down from the bookstore and parallel parked. He hadn't done that for quite a spell. In the city he parked in large lots or garages, not on the streets. People smiled and nodded as he passed them on the sidewalk. Another thing he liked about small towns.

Several customers preceded him into the bookstore. Maybe that meant he'd have time to do some investigating on his own without Ellie Benton seeing him. He took a few minutes to survey the layout of the store. Tables of bargain books greeted him at the front along with gifts items and a special display of new books. Upon closer examination, he discovered they were all Christian inspirational novels and books. How had he missed that? This was an independent Christian bookstore, and that warmed his heart. Not many stores like this existed anymore.

With a bit of trepidation, he headed straight for the fiction section and perused the shelves. There among the some of the best writers he knew, sat three copies of his latest Jake Reed novels, *Run to Survive.*

So, she did carry his books. In fact, the more he investigated, the more books from inspirational writers he found. He had to chuckle at the names. Mrs. Benton kept him in pretty good company.

"Mr. Hill, so nice to see you this morning."

He spun around to find the store owner herself grinning from ear to ear. He'd been so absorbed in what he was doing that he hadn't heard her approach. "Er...huh...good morning, Mrs. Benton."

Her laughter echoed her soft southern drawl. "I'm sorry. I didn't mean to startle you. Can I help you with something?"

"Hmm, not really, I was browsing the books to see what you have." Now he'd have to buy a book from her. "Going to buy a book for my mother. She loves to read and you have a great selection here."

Pink tinged her cheeks as she beamed a smile that lit up her face. "Wonderful. I'm sure you'll find something. Let me know if I can help you in anyway, but please call me Ellie. That's what everyone in town does."

"I will, Mrs. Benton . . . I mean, Ellie. Thank you." He waited until she had disappeared around the end of the row and turned back to the books. His mother liked mystery and suspense, but not the intense kind Brandilyn Collins wrote. She said those kept her awake at night. Mom wouldn't even read his books for the same reason.

He was here in the H section, so he pulled out a Dee Henderson book titled *Taken* and read the blurb. This mom would like. He tucked it under his arm and made his way to the check-out register.

Another woman manned the register, and he didn't see Ellie Benton anywhere. He paid for the book and glanced around, but the store owner was still nowhere in sight. His mission was accomplished, so it didn't really matter whether he saw her again or not.

A few minutes later he pulled out of the parking space and decided to drive around for a little while longer. He had told Jolie he'd be gone at least an hour and he had half of that left. He'd left Jake Reed fighting for his life, but the man would survive. Maybe he'd send Jake to a small town like Weinberg on his next mission.

When he passed the church, his thoughts returned to Jolie. She was a woman who had a good head on her shoulders, a wonderful sense of humor and good looks to boot. Maybe he could ask her to join him for lunch next Sunday after church. That should start a few tongues a wagging and heads a nodding. Then he scolded himself. It was part of a game, but was it fair to let Mrs. Burns and her friends think their plans were working? Especially since he actually enjoyed Jolie's company.

Chapter 8

*O*n Friday morning, Clay came downstairs and stayed for breakfast. Jolie was busy with diners and had no time to speak to him, but she was well aware of his presence every minute he lingered. This morning he sat at the same table as Charley, Ava Lou, and Darlene and had them laughing and falling all over themselves to get his attention.

Jolie turned her back to them and went to the registration desk to pick up the signs she'd designed for the garden club banner. She tapped the papers on her fingers, debating whether to go in now and hand it to them while he sat there or to wait until the ladies prepared to leave.

They solved the dilemma for her when Charley strutted into the foyer, her shoulders back and her head held high. "I tell you, Jolene Burns, you better latch on to that young man. He's a real keeper."

Ava Lou and Darlene joined her nodding their heads in agreement. Jolie handed Darlene the folder with the designs. "I'm glad you like him, but he's not going to be here long enough for anything more than friendly exchanges."

Darlene held the folder, ready to open it. "Well, if you ask me, you two looked like you were having a fine time Wednesday night at supper."

"It was nice." He had played the game well for the benefit of the ladies.

"Oh, these are wonderful! You did a great job. I'll get them right over to the sign shop and have the banners made." She held the folder out for Charley and Ava Lou to see.

"I think they look great as well. You're very talented, Jolie."

Clay's voice rang out behind them. Jolie jumped and the ladies laughed.

"We'll be going now. Want to get these to the shop." Darlene waved he folder. "Have fun you two." She giggled and joined Charley and Ava Lou to leave.

After the door closed behind the three women, Clay lingered at her desk. "I remember you telling me you were graphic artist and designer in Houston before coming home. You must have designed the sign out front."

"I did. I do love creating logos and designs for various and sundry companies and organizations." This was certainly a turnaround from yesterday morning when he dashed back to his room for breakfast and stayed there most of the morning.

"If that one you just gave Mrs. Williams is any indication, you're quite good, but that isn't what I want to talk about right now. How busy are Sundays when you have guests?"

What a strange question. "Not too busy after breakfast. We end the buffet early on Sundays and encourage our guests to attend church. Many of them do, but some simply go back to their rooms and get ready for whatever else they may do that day."

"I see. Well then, would you join me for church and dinner after? I would like to hear your pastor, and since we both have to eat, I thought maybe you'd dine with me. That would really give the ladies something to chew on."

A knot formed in Jolie's stomach and twisted her insides. He'd asked her out, but it was only to carry on their charade. Still, she had agreed to it, so there was no reason not to go with him. She only had to remember this was not real and he would be leaving in seven weeks.

"Yes, it would, and I'd like to have dinner with you. Do you want to meet us at the church? Mom and I go for the Bible study classes as well, but you don't have to do that."

"No, I'd enjoy that. I'm a member of a singles department at my church in Dallas. What time will you leave?"

"Probably around a quarter to nine. Classes

start at nine-fifteen so that will give us time to get there and have coffee."

"Sounds good to me." He grinned and stepped back. "I'll leave you now as I know you have to get ready for the guests who'll be arriving later as well as help your mom with preparations for lunch. I'll work up in my room, but I'll be down later to eat."

He tipped his fingers to his forehead and jogged up the stairs.

Now that was some exchange. He actually wanted to attend the Bible class. Jolie chuckled. She couldn't wait to see the expressions on the faces of the other members when they realized her guest had joined her for church. All the women would be bowled over by his good looks and charm. It sure hadn't taken long for Clay to grab her interest.

~

The screen remained blank. Clay's fingers rested on the keyboard, but no words came forth. His mind focused on a delightful young woman downstairs helping her mother prepare the noonday meal.

Friday meant chicken pot pie on the menu, and he'd already heard from several others as to how good it was. Even now heavenly aromas wafted up from the kitchen all the way to his third floor room. Must be the ventilating system, but whatever or wherever was, it started a rumble in his stomach.

Jolie had said she'd go to church with him, but maybe he should have asked her to go out tomorrow night. He'd seen a movie theater complex out at the edge of town that showed four movies at one time, but maybe she'd seen them all.

Too late now, and if he didn't get busy with this chapter, he wouldn't have time to do anything else. He'd been in town four full days and had managed only three full chapters in that time. He'd have to do double time in order to get thirty-five to forty finished, revised and self-edited in the next seven weeks.

He read back over what he'd written and the words for the next scene emerged. For the next hour, his fingers flew over the keyboard and he completed the scene and sent Jake off on another mission. Another chapter came to an end.

The alarm on his phone chirped. Time for a break and lunch. He turned off the alarm and stretched his arms over his head. His policy of taking a ten minute break every hour helped keep him from aching all over from sitting so long.

After washing up, he combed his hair back in place. It usually stood up in all directions after a writing session because of the number of times he ran his fingers over and through it. Satisfied that he looked decent again, Clay headed down to the tearoom.

Chatter and noise of silverware and glasses told him lunch was well underway. Jolie hailed him from inside the room and hurried to him with a menu in hand.

"Come on in. I saved a table for you back

there. Mom's friends aren't here yet, so you'll have a little peace."

Her smile lit up his heart. He'd follow her anywhere. Oops. He better get his thoughts elsewhere. After he was seated, he took the offered menu in hand. "Thanks, but I think I want the pot pie everyone talks about. I'll look through this for a dessert though. Oh, and water is all I need to drink."

"I'll get right on it." She left the table and stopped to speak to a young woman holding a tray of food. The girl glanced in his direction and nodded. He recognized her as Hayley, one of the waitresses who helped in the tearoom.

In a few minutes she was beside him with a glass of water. "Here you go, Mr. Hill. I'll have your pot pie out shortly." Then she headed to another table.

Laughter near the front caught his attention and he realized Charley and Darlene had arrived. Neither Ava nor Ellie was with them. Jolie led them to a table on the other side of the room, and he silently thanked her. Maybe he could eat in peace today.

He gazed about the room and admired once again the old-fashioned look of the place. Predominant colors were those of the bluebonnet for which the inn had been named. Linen napkins and tablecloths may be more expensive for them to use than paper, but they added to the charm of the tearoom. The eclectic use of mismatched china plates and other dishes intrigued him as well.

This must have been a fine old home in its day, and it certainly made for a beautiful bed and breakfast. Jolie had said the weekend guests would most likely arrive in the afternoon, but with him in the only room on the third floor and surrounded by attic, he shouldn't be bothered by noise.

He drummed his fingers on the table top. It wasn't noise that would bother him, but the face of the pretty lady speaking to customers and showing them to tables.

His pot pie arrived and the first taste assured him it was as good as people had said. He ate and observed the people around him. The friendly smiles of those who enjoyed their meal and the laughter from various tables enhanced the family atmosphere of the tearoom.

Charley spotted him and waved across the room before she nudged Darlene who swiveled her head around to see him. She smiled and waved too. He returned the greeting and hoped they wouldn't come to his table.

They didn't and he finished his meal. He left the amount for the lunch and a tip on the table and ambled to the exit. Jolie stopped him in the foyer.

"I thought I'd warn you. Charley is talking about asking you to help them with the Weinberg Garden Club booth at the Bluebonnet Fair next week."

Clay chuckled and shook his head. "Now what could I do to help them?"

Her blue eyes twinkled with delight. "Oh, you'd be surprised what they could cook up for you to do. Carrying tables and flats of bedding plants and potted plants would be starters."

"I think I could handle that. What is the fair all about anyway?" He'd heard of so many of these spring festivals and fairs in Texas but had never attended one.

"Lots of decorated booths with all types of crafts, foods, clothes, garden stuff, and even furniture. Just about anything you could want is available."

"Sounds like fun. I look forward to it. Are you attending with anyone?" Maybe that would give them more time together.

"Well, I'm working the booth for Mom, but…" She leaned forward with a teasing look about her and whispered, "Since her friends are trying to get us together, let's see what they come up with. If they don't, I'll be finished at the booth by ten or so."

"Sounds like a plan to me. I'll wait and see what they want me to do that morning."

Before they could plan anything else, Charley and Darlene swept into the foyer. Charlene waved her hand. "There you are! Just the man we wanted to see. Right, Darlene?"

"Oh my, yes. We wanted to ask if you'd be so kind as to help us get our booth set up at the Bluebonnet Fair. It's a week from tomorrow you know."

They sure hadn't wasted any time. He grinned at Jolie and winked. "I'd be glad to help you, Ladies. Just let me know where and when."

"See, I told you he would." Charley poked Darlene in the side with her elbow. "Be at my place by seven-thirty. We plan to open the booth at eight-thirty, so we'll have an hour to get set up."

"All right, you can count on me."

Darlene tilted her head. "You'll be helping in the booth first thing, too, won't you, Jolie?"

"Yes, ma'am, I'll be there to help you open up soon as I finish breakfast here."

Jolie grinned at Clay behind Charley and Darlene who had turned and were focused on him, not her.

The two women scurried to leave, their heads together in conversation.

Jolie laughed and shook her head. "I told you so."

"Yes, you did, and thanks for warning me." He pulled the key to his room from his pocket. "I'm going back up now and so some more wri . . . work on my project."

He didn't take the steps two at a time as he usually did. He scolded himself once again. Keeping her in the dark about his project was being deceptive. Since he trusted her discretion now that he knew her little better, he should tell her the truth. He jammed the key into the old-fashioned lock. On Sunday he'd tell her what he was really doing in Weinberg.

With that decision behind him, Clay sat at his computer and devised new perils for his hero.

Chapter 9

With an almost full house of guests, Jolie stayed busy helping her mother keep things running smoothly. Yesterday, she didn't have any time to herself until after the tearoom closed. She'd seen little of Clay as he'd kept to his room most of the day. Must be some big project to keep him closed up in his room on a beautiful spring Saturday.

She pulled out a dress and a pair of slacks from her closet and held them up. Casual or Sunday best? Most of the girls her age wore dress slacks and jackets to church, but Jolie wore those all week. She opted for the blue dress with three quarter sleeves and a full skirt. She liked dressing up a little more for church, and with a dress, she'd wear higher heels.

Instead of a necklace, she selected a blue print

infinity scarf around her neck and blue dangle ear clips. All her friends had their ears pierced as pre-teens, but Jolie had opted out of that and was glad after all the trouble the others had.

At a quarter to nine, she stepped into the foyer and found Clay descending the stairs. Promptness, another thing she admired in others. Six days, and he hadn't disappointed her yet. Honest, clean cut, a Christian, on time, and handsome. All the things she'd had on her list of what she'd look for in a man before Mark Hartley swept her off her feet. She shoved that image out of her mind and headed for the front entry way.

Clay waited for her by the desk. She smiled and said, "Good morning. I see you're right on time."

"Of course." He grinned and joined her to walk to the back entrance. "I'm not one to keep a lady waiting."

When they arrived at the church minutes later, Jolie and Clay entered the foyer. She spotted her mother and friends over to the side, their heads bobbing in conversation. Jolie pulled Clay into the stairway leading to the second floor where the Singles Bible Class met.

Jolie bounded up the steps. Once on the second floor, she halted and waited for Clay to catch up. "I'm sorry, but I didn't want Mom and her friends to delay our getting up to class. They would've talked our arms off if they had seen us."

He breathed deeply and exhaled. "I wondered

why you took off in such a hurry."

"I didn't want to hear any more of their plans and hints this morning. I'm hoping we can avoid them during church as well." She nodded toward a door nearby. "Come on, let's go into class."

Just as she'd expected, people greeted them warmly, ladies first of course. She had to admit, he took it all in stride as though he might be used to people crowding around him. Probably his charm and good looks wowed them as well as his being a new male in town.

She poured a cup of coffee and picked up a donut hole before finding a seat. One of the girls leaned over Jolie's shoulders. "Where in the world has that hunk of a man been hiding? Oh, you're so lucky to have him staying at the inn where you can see him every day." She rolled her eyes in his direction. Without waiting for Jolie's comment or answer, the woman found a seat two rows ahead.

Jolie sipped her coffee and soaked in the sight of Clay in animated conversation with two of the single men in the department. They both had been two years behind Jolie in school, and it amused her now to see them as grown men. From their gestures and facial expressions, they must be talking sports and since it was spring, most likely baseball or golf.

A few minutes later Clay sauntered over to the chair she had saved for him. "Thanks for the seat. Met some nice young men over there."

"And I bet you were talking sports."

Clay grinned. "How did you know? Ron told me you have a great golf course, and we're going to play a round someday soon."

Before she could respond, the teacher stood and led them in prayer. All through the lesson, Jolie listened, but didn't really hear everything he said. She kept stealing glances at Clay. He was handsome, friendly, a Christian, and was fun to be with, so why did she hesitate to let herself have feelings for him?

Nope, she'd gone that route before. A man had to do more than simply say he liked having her by his side and do more than giving her a ring with empty promises. She bit her lip and turned her attention to the teacher. In a little over seven weeks, he'd be gone back to the city and his life there. He didn't have room in his life for a small town girl who helped manage a bed and breakfast.

After the lesson ended and they had exchanged a few words with others who asked Clay to be sure and come back, he led her to the hallway and downstairs to the sanctuary. They hurried inside to avoid her mother and took seats in a pew toward the back. Jolie bit back a chuckle when her mother and friends rushed in at the last minute to find their places near the front.

Jolie nudged Clay. "They must have been out there looking for us. I'm glad we got out of class before they did. Their curiosity must be at a peak because I told Mom we were going to lunch after church."

"I can imagine their surprise. Do you want to meet them after, or make a dash for the car and get going before they realize we're gone?"

They stood to sing the first praise number, and she gazed up at him. "Let's run for it and have time for ourselves. They'll probably be waiting back at the inn, so we can enjoy ourselves in peace." Heat rose in her cheeks, and she cringed. That did not come out the way she meant for it to sound.

"Sounds like a plan to me."

~

After dinner where he and Jolie had talked about everything, Clay suggested a drive in the countryside to see the bluebonnets now blooming at their peak. He would tell her his true reason for being in Weinberg somewhere amid the flowers.

"I love driving out here on the back roads this time of the year. The fields are a solid blanket of blue."

Clay turned onto a dirt road between two fields. "I don't know where this leads, but we can stop and take a few pictures." With her blue eyes and the darker blue in the dress she wore today, he'd have a picture to remember.

He stopped the car by a fence and went around to open her door. "This looks like as good a place as any."

She slid from the seat and surveyed the field of blue that stretched for miles in all directions. Her heart swelled with pride at the beauty of the state flower that gave the inn its name. "Hmm, this looks like it may be private property. Maybe we should find somewhere else."

"If we stay right here at the fence, we should be okay." He climbed over the low cedar fence and held out his hand to help her over.

Her feet and ankles disappeared into the blooms spread over the ground. Careful not to crush any of the flowers, she ventured a few feet away. "This is beautiful, but let's hurry and then get out of here. I can just see an angry farmer storming out here with his shotgun ready to blast."

Clay aimed his camera at her. "Wow, you do have an imagination, but these make a beautiful backdrop."

After a few poses, he moved to her side. "Now for a selfie." He wrapped his arm around her shoulder and pulled her close. After a few poses, he lowered the camera, but kept his arm around her. Her face, so close to his, was irresistible. He leaned down until his lips met hers. She didn't pull away, and his arm tightened around her.

When he held her closer and attempted to deepen the kiss, she pushed against his chest. "I...I can't do this. It's too soon."

He dropped his arms to his side. "I'm sorry, Jolie. I couldn't resist with you so close. If it's too soon for you, I can wait." He grinned and caressed her cheek. "Maybe by the end of the two months I can try again." His prayer would be not to have to wait that long. This beautiful woman had opened a longing in his heart he thought had disappeared forever.

Even as he considered a future with her, the time had come for the truth. He could trust her with his secret . . . which may not be a secret much longer if Ellie Benton's expression this morning meant what he thought it did.

"It's time to go." She fled back to the car and climbed in.

Once Clay joined her in the car, he didn't start the engine right away. She furrowed her brow and stared at him. "Aren't we leaving?"

"Not just yet. I have something to tell you about why I'm here and staying at the inn." He paused and cleared his throat. "Hmm, my real name is Clayton Hill, but many more people know me as Clive Hendrix, author of the Jake Reed spy thrillers."

Her blank expression unnerved him. She had no clue. "I'm a writer and I'm here to work on my next novel and meet my deadline."

"Oh, I see. That's what your project is then . . . a novel." Her expression hadn't changed.

"Yes, and you have no idea who Clive Hendrix is."

Pink filled her face. "No, I'm sorry, I don't. Are they secular or Christian?"

He loved the way she blushed so easily. "They're Christian and Ellie Benton carries them at her store. I'm telling you because I think Ellie may have recognized me and will start telling the world. I didn't want you to find out from her."

An impish smile lit her face. "The ladies' are going to have a field day with this."

"I imagine they will, and I need you to sort of run interference for me. I do need the time and privacy to get this novel finished and to my editor." Not to mention the fact that thoughts of her interfered more than the idea of being recognized.

"Ellie will be telling everyone who comes into her store that you're here in town. You may have to take more meals in your room and in the next town."

"Maybe so, but can we keep up our charade as well? Let them believe we're together?" Then maybe it would be real by the end of his stay.

"I don't know, Clay. This business of your being a well-known author is something I'll have to think about and digest."

His heart plummeted, but he'd go along with whatever made her comfortable. He turned the key in the ignition and started the motor, then glanced at her and a smiled played about her lips.

"Regardless of what we do, we can't hurt mother's friends. Let's wait and see what happens in the next few hours. It'll be interesting to see how they let us know that they know who you are."

The day turned even brighter and more beautiful than it already was. He'd wait as long as it took for her to develop any feelings at all for him. No woman had ever affected him like Jolene Burns, and he had to come up with a plan to keep her in his life even after he finished his book.

When they neared the inn, Jolie shook her head. "I just happened to think. Mom's friend, Andy is coming back into town later today. He's an avid reader, and he might be a fan of yours. So, if the ladies haven't recognized you, he probably will."

"Okay, but who is this Andy?"

"He and Mom were friends long ago, but both have lost their spouses and they have re-connected since he moved back to Weinberg after his retirement. He's been in Houston working with his son. He turned his company over to him last fall, but goes back every month for a few days to check on things. I think he just wants to keep his hand in the business, and his son doesn't seem to mind."

"I see. Well, I look forward to meeting him." He turned into the drive at the inn and drove around to the back parking lot.

If he survived the weeks ahead and finished his book, he'd find a way to her heart. If it meant moving to Weinberg, he would because he'd do anything to be close to Jolie. Books can be written anywhere.

Chapter 10

*J*olie considered all that Clay told her about his writing. After he explained what his books were about, she didn't feel so guilty at not recognizing his name. Spy thrillers were not on her list of books to read. However, she might pick one up simply to see if his writing was any good.

Mom wouldn't know him from Adam either, but if Ellie said he was a celebrity, then Mom would be all excited about his staying at the inn. Funny, but his own mother didn't read his books either.

When they pulled into a space in the parking lot, Jolie spotted Andy Benefield's red SUV in the drive. "Now you'll get to meet Andy. I think you'll like him. He sorta reminds me of Andy Griffith, not as Andy Taylor of Mayberry, but of that lawyer, Matlock."

"My mother loved that show and wanted to know why I didn't write about lawyers instead of spies." Clay parked and opened his door and came around to assist Jolie.

Andy came down the back steps. "Hey, you two, I'm glad you're back. The ladies didn't hear the car, but I've been looking for you."

He enveloped Jolie in a hug then stepped back and extended is hand to Clay. "Name's Andy Benefield and I know who you are. That's why I came to meet you first."

"We figured Ellie had recognized me and told Mrs. Burns and her friends."

"That she did. I would have recognized you as soon as I met you because I've read all your books and your picture is on the back covers. Anyway, I wanted to warn you."

"Thanks, Mr. Benefield. I appreciate it and thanks for reading my books. We weren't sure how to handle the ladies."

Andy gripped Clay's shoulder. "Boy, just act surprised that they know, and you'll give them more excitement than they've had since the fire in the kitchen when they were remodeling."

Jolie cringed when Clay peered at her with questions filling his eyes. "I'll tell you all about it sometime. Long story."

The back door burst open and Mom almost fell down the stairs in her excitement. "You're back. Hurry on in here. We want to talk to both of you." She pivoted and disappeared through the door.

Andy laughed and slapped Clay on the back. "Time to face the music. They have a plan, but don't feel guilty if you don't want to go along with it."

A plan? Jolie's head spun with all the ideas her mother and friends could be hatching or had hatched. She followed Clay and Andy inside.

The voices of her mother and Charley carried into the hallway and drew the three of them to the sitting area by the tearoom.

When Andy entered with Clay, the ladies clamped their mouths shut for a moment and stared at Clay. Then Ellie Benton jumped and clasped her hands to her chest. "It *is* you. Just like your picture on the back of your book."

Charley shook her head and pointed a finger at Jolie. "You should have suspected something young lady." Next she pointed at Clay. "And you. Being holed up for a project indeed. Writing your new book is more like it, not that I've read any of yours."

"Charley, I had no idea until he told me earlier this afternoon."

Ellen pushed Jolie aside and stood in front of Clay with a look of pure adoration on her face. "None of that matters now. We have a celebrity of sorts in our town and we need to do something about it. And for your information, I have read your books and they are wonderful. I love Jake Reed."

"Thank you, Mrs. Benton. I appreciate your kind words, but I came to Weinberg so I wouldn't have any distractions and could make the deadline on this latest book."

Clay spoke to Ellie with nothing but kindness in his voice and manner, and Jolie respected him for that, but her hands clenched into fists at this new development. She didn't need another fiasco like had happened with Mark.

Ellie picked up a copy of his book. "I do understand that, but it's not every week we have a noted author to visit our fair town. We have a favor to ask of you and of Jolie."

Jolie glanced at her mother who merely shrugged her shoulders. Charley kept her eyes everywhere else but in contact with Jolie's.

Clay's eyebrows rose. "And what may that be, Mrs. Benton?"

"We . . . I . . . no, we all would like for you to have a book signing at my store. We need Jolie to make the flyers to announce it and to put an announcement in the *Gazette.* If you'll do just one, we promise to leave you alone to finish your book."

Jolie made no comment. If Clay agreed to do the book signing, then everyone in town would know his identity and invade the tearoom to catch a glimpse of him. Neither of them would have much peace.

Clay grinned and shook his head. "Okay, Mrs. Benton. I'll do the book-signing for you. When do you want to do it?"

Ellie squealed in delight, and Mom and Charley hugged each other. Jolie should have known he'd grant their request. He was too nice a guy not too. Maybe she ought to pick up one of those books and read it before the signing.

"Well, I have to order enough books first, get all the publicity out, and plan a schedule for the day. It usually takes two weeks to get the books, but maybe I can put in a rush order, and we can have them here for a signing the Saturday after the Bluebonnet Fair. If we'd known sooner, we could have made it a part of the fair with so many people in town for that."

Ellie rattled on like an old jalopy with her plans and ideas with Mom and Charley making a few choice comments here and there. Jolie's heart flip-flopped. This meant being in the public eye again, and that was something she didn't care to experience. Jolie finally held up her hand.

"Whoa there, all y'all. You're going way too fast with this."

Mom narrowed her eyes at Jolie. "You *are* going to help us aren't you?"

"Yes, I will, but I do think it's time to slow down and take things one at a time rather than spewing out a bunch of stuff."

Clay linked arms with her. "It's okay, Jolie. If she thinks she can have it all done in two weeks, that's fine with me. All I have to do is show up. Two or three hours isn't so much that I can't do something to help Mrs. Benton."

"You're supposed to call me Ellie 'cause everyone else in town does." She scolded but clasped her hands to her chest once more. "This is going to be the best book signing this town has ever seen." Pure joy laced her words.

After what she'd just witnessed, Jolie had no doubts about Ellie's prediction. After all they'd done for Mom, Jolie would make sure Ellie had everything she needed. "All right, Ellie. Come up with your ideas about publicity and I'll do the same. We want to get those flyers out soon as possible."

"Oh, I'll go get started on that right now." She grabbed Charley's arm. "Come on. Let's go get Ava Lou and Darlene and start planning."

Clay shook Andy's hand again. "It's been nice to meet you, and I hope you'll be around for the big event."

Andy roared with laughter. "Son, this is one thing I wouldn't miss for a million dollars. When those ladies get their teeth into something, the rest of the world had better watch out."

Mom hugged Jolie. "I'm so glad you're not angry with the girls. They were so excited when they found out who Clay really is." Then she grabbed Clay's hand. "And thank you for going along with the idea. It means a lot to Ellie."

"I don't mind, and if it'll help the bookstore, then it'll be worth the time. Now if you'll excuse me, I need to get upstairs and see what else I can find for Jake Reed to get into."

Andy and her mother locked arms and headed for the kitchen for a snack or whatever, and Jolie sighed. Getting involved with someone else in the limelight had not been on her list of things to do. Her hand touched her lips. The kiss had seemed real, but then so had Mark's. She shivered and wrapped her arms around her chest. This time she'd use a lot more caution and treat this new project with the ladies as a business deal and nothing else.

~

Clay tromped up to his room. His cover had been blown. He'd have to call his agent and his editor to let them know what was going on and where he'd come to write. He opened the door to his room and sauntered to the chair by the window and slumped into it. If the ladies kept their promise and let this be the only time to be public with his writing, he'd still have plenty of time to finish the book.

His main concern for the moment had to be Jolie. He'd been somewhat miffed that she hadn't recognized his name, especially being from Houston. Bookstores carried his books and big posters with his name and latest releases adorned many of their walls, but she was still clueless as to who he was and what he wrote.

A change in attitude resulting in coolness came over her while Ellie went on about the book signing event. A veil had fallen over her eyes and the sparkle had disappeared. He needed her help to get through the next two weeks. He pushed up from his slump. Face the facts. He didn't need her help; he wanted her help for the next two months, not just the two weeks.

With a sigh for the inevitable he called his agent.

Her answer came after the second ring. "Clay, I've been waiting to hear from you. How is the book coming?"

"Got a good start. I'll send you the first chapters so you can check them out."

"Wonderful, but I wish you'd tell me where you are." The pout in her voice was clear.

"I'm in Weinberg, Texas at a bed and breakfast. Although I used my own name, the bookstore owner here recognized me and now wants to do a book signing in two weeks."

Anne's laughter filled the airwaves. "That's a good one. So much for trying to be incognito. Do you mind if I come down there for the signing?"

"No, that's why I called. I thought you might want to be in on it. I'll check to see if they have a room available for you that weekend. You'll really like the Bluebonnet Inn. Very friendly and nice people."

"Sounds like a great plan to me. Let's see, I can leave Dallas on Friday and get there to spend Friday night and Saturday night and come home on Sunday. I'll clear my calendar and see you then."

"Okay. I'll let you know about the room."

Clay hit end and covered his eyes with the back of his hand still holding the phone. No, the ladies wouldn't be interfering with his writing, but he couldn't say the same for one Jolene Burns who'd be on his mind more than the exploits of Jake Reed. Something had gone out of Jolie's eyes in the last hour, and he'd spend the rest of however long it took to get it back and see those blue eyes filled with joy once again.

Chapter 11

*T*he Saturday for the Bluebonnet Fair arrived, and Clay looked forward to helping the ladies with their booth. When he went down to breakfast that morning, inn guests as well as other fair goers filled the room even though he had arrived only ten minutes after serving had begun.

Jolie and the two girls taking care of guests had no time for any visiting as they did on week-day mornings. Clay filled a plate, found a tray, and headed back to his room. He tried to catch Jolie's attention, but she never looked his way.

Whatever had happened last Sunday after she learned who he was had caused her to avoid him as much as possible this past week. The only contact he had was when she had a message to relay to him about the book signing next weekend and to let him know his agent had booked a room.

He spotted Mrs. Burns speaking with a guest and waited nearby until the guest left. "Mrs. Burns, may I have a minute of your time?"

She glanced back at the kitchen. "Yes, I think I can spare a few more away from filling the buffet. Looks like everyone is served and eating. What can I do for you?"

"It's about Jolie. We were getting along so well, and then last Sunday after she learned who I was, she turned on a deep freeze. She's avoided me all week. We had made plans, but now she's not even talking to me."

Mrs. Burns frowned and bit her lip. "I'm not sure what or how much to say. She came out of a relationship that went sour when she came here to help me with the inn. My friends and I have been doing everything we could think of to bring her out of the doldrums, and we thought we'd succeeded when she began going out with you. She actually laughed and smiled for the first time in ages."

Well, that part of their plan worked, but something had gone wrong. "I really enjoy our time together. She's funny, smart, and loves beautiful things. I have some great shots of her in the bluebonnets we took last Sunday. I want to see that pure joy back in her eyes."

"Oh, Clay, that's the best news I've heard. I did notice you weren't around as much, but I figured it had to do with your deadline and trying to get ready for the book-signing."

Clay shook his head. "Don't worry about that. All I have to do is show up for the signing. From what Ellie and Ava Lou have told me this week, they have it all planned and waiting for the books to arrive. The signs are in the window, and I've seen a few around town."

"Oh, I do hope that hasn't created a problem for you."

"No, it hasn't. I'll admit I have to sign a few books every time I eat supper in town, but that's not so bad, and I enjoy getting to know my readers." And that was the truth. Satisfied readers were what kept the royalties coming in. They didn't take away from his writing time nearly as much as Jolie did.

"I'm so glad." She glanced at his hands. "Oh, I see you have a tray. Are you going back up to your room?"

"Yes, I thought I might get finished quicker in my room. I promised to help the ladies with their booth. I'm supposed to meet Charley and Darlene to load their supplies on Charley's truck and then help unload at the booth."

"Yes, and that was so sweet of you." She shooed him with her hands. "Now get on with you so you won't be late. I'm going back to help Bertha. We'll work this out with Jolie yet."

He trudged up the stairs to his room and made fresh coffee to go with his now cold eggs and biscuit. A few seconds in the microwave took care of that. Somehow, today he'd have to get Jolie alone and force her to tell him what had happened. Maybe not force her, but at least try to get some answers. Although Mrs. Burns had given him a little information, he still needed more. This past week with her evasive behavior hurt more than he thought possible.

Half an hour later, he returned the tray and dishes downstairs and headed out for Charley's place. When he arrived, Charley had all the bedding plants in flats and ready to load onto her truck along with two banners, the canopy and the tables for the booth. However, the lady herself was nowhere in sight.

Ava arrived with the potted plants that included geraniums, gerbera daisies, and begonias.

"Ava, those plants are really pretty. A great variety of color in the daisies and begonias."

"Now, how do you know the names of these flowers? Most men wouldn't know a zinnia from a violet."

"That's my mother's doing. She loves to garden and had has all these in her yard in Oklahoma as well as tulips and daffodils and lots of rose bushes." Clay lifted a large flat of bedding plants and slid them onto the truck bed.

Ava Lou smiled and clapped her hands. "I like that mother of yours. A lady after my own heart. Too bad she lives all the way up in Oklahoma."

"Yeah, I miss her. I usually try to make it up to Tulsa in the spring. It's almost as pretty there as the bluebonnets are here." Mom would say prettier, but he wasn't about to tell the ladies something like that.

Charley returned with an armful of potted plants. "Good morning, Clay. These are the last of the ones we potted last night."

After ten minutes they had the truck loaded and ready to take to the fairgrounds where they would meet Darlene. They should have just enough time to get it set up and ready for the eight o'clock ribbon cutting and opening. Jolie had said she'd be there later, but if she worked the booth, he'd have no time to visit with her.

Clay helped Charley put up the canopy in the garden club book spot. "Charley, how long is Jolie supposed to work the booth this morning?"

Charley grinned and snapped a pole into a loop. "Not sure. Her momma is coming to relieve her when she gets through with the guests at the inn, so I'd guess an hour or two. Which reminds me, I haven't seen the two of you together much this week."

"You're right because we haven't been together. That's what I hope to remedy today."

"Glad to hear it. I like seeing the two of you having fun." Charley straightened the last post. "Now let's get that banner hanging."

He fastened the last corner of the loop and a familiar voice called out to him. He turned and almost fell off his ladder. His agent strode toward him. "Anne! What are you doing here this weekend? The book-signing is next Saturday. I booked your room for then"

"I know, but I read about this fair online and decided to come see it for myself. All the hotels around are full this weekend, but I found one only forty-five minutes away. Came down last night to surprise you today. I want to meet all these ladies who talked you into the event next week."

Charley and Ava Lou stood with their mouths gaping open and Darlene hugged an apron to her chest. Clay pointed toward them. These are my new friends, Charley, Ava Lou, and Darlene. Ladies, this is my agent, Anne Holcomb."

Clay grinned as Anne turned on her charm and had the ladies in awe with her winsome smile and interest in their project. Clay patted Anne's back. "I'll leave you to get more acquainted. If you want me, I'll be back at the inn . . . working."

Charley placed her hands on her hips and frowned. "You do plan to come back, don't you?"

"Of course I do. Gotta see what all these booths have to offer. Be back in a couple of hours." He waved and jogged back to his car. All around booths finished booths displayed and crafts, foods, and antiques to lure fair goers to come visit. A crowd gathered at the front entrance where the mayor and other citizens waited to cut the ribbon to open the two-day event.

Clay checked his watch. Five minutes until opening. He'd definitely be back by ten, but until then he'd see what else could happen to Jake. One of these days he'd have to try plotting it all out in advance, but right now he enjoyed the surprises his hero had in store for him as the story moved along.

~

Jolie spotted Clay heading toward his car. She slipped behind a tree and waited until he entered the street back to the inn before she hurried down the rows to the garden club booth. When she neared the booth, a strange woman stood conversing with Charley, Ava Lou and Darlene.

Charley waved at Jolie. "Come on over here, girl. We got somebody you need to meet."

Curiosity drew Jolie to walk a little faster. The woman turned with a smile as bright as sunshine on her lips. Who in the world was this? Jolie had never seen her in Weinberg before.

When she reached the booth, Charley grabbed her arm. "Come on and meet Anne Holcomb. She's Clay's . . . er . . . uh . . . Clive's agent."

Clay's agent? What was she doing here this Saturday? "I'm Jolene Burns. My mom owns the inn where Clay is staying."

Anne raised her eyebrows and extended her hand in greeting. "I'm so glad to meet you. I'm staying at your inn next Saturday, and I've heard a lot about you from these ladies. It's really nice of you to help them."

"Actually, I'm doing it for my mother. She had to stay back at the inn this morning, so I'm taking her place until she can get here."

Anne waved her hand in the air. "Oh, I'm not talking about that. I mean the banner you designed, the pamphlet and the publicity for the book signing next week. Excellent work. I'm sure it'll help draw large crowds to the booth and to the signing."

"Thank you, but like you said, your reservation is for next week, and our rooms are all filled."

"I'm aware of that, so I have a room in the next town. Not too long a drive. I'm here to check out the town and see if there's anything I can do to help Mrs. Benton with the book signing next week. I understand she'll be here in the booth later."

"Yes, she has the book store open for those who may want to drop in for books. My mother will be here later as well, so you'll get to meet her."

Charley and Ava Lou latched on to Anne again and told her what more of what they planned for the signing.

Jolie put her hands to use and arrange the flowers by color and kind. Apparently the ladies had forgotten the little plants when Anne showed up, but how did she get into the fair before opening? No time to wonder about that.

A roar went up by the front gate which meant they were now open and the crowds would come streaming through. If the number of cars already filling the lots was any indication, they might break a few records for attendance.

Anne left, but said she'd be back after checking out some of the other vendors. Jolie planned to be gone before then unless her mother arrived late. This was not the morning she cared to deal with

Clay's agent. Andy had already scolded her for avoiding Clay all week.

Jolie sighed and sat down at the table with the cash box and receipt book. She inserted the credit app into the USB port of the tablet and prepared for the first few customers. As much as she'd tried to explain to Mom that there was too much to do to prepare for today to take a lot of time to visit or go anywhere with Clay, Mom had fussed and nagged Jolie to quit hiding and go back to what she'd been doing the past week.

That Jolie couldn't do. How could she have let herself be so drawn to him in less than seven days? People couldn't fall for each other that quick. A reality check reminded her that she'd done it before and how badly it had turned out. If she spent the next two months getting to know him and growing closer to him, he'd only up and leave and go back to his world of books and fame. The last thing she wanted was to be in anybody's spotlight, no matter how nice they might be on the outside.

These next seven or so weeks would be the hardest she'd spent in a long time.

Chapter 12

*J*olie managed to leave the fair grounds and get back to the inn before Clay came back. She sat in her room with one of his books. The picture on the back was a good likeness, and she ran her fingertips over the image. He wasn't as well-known as Mark had been, but she looked him up on Google and found him.

So much she didn't know about Clayton Hill. The website was more about Clive Hendricks than Clay or was it all about Clay? She read the information again and realized what she read did coincide with some of what Clay had told her.

His website listed a large number of books, and she had clicked on one to find out more about it. Rather than risk a trip to the bookstore and getting grilled for information by Ellie, she called

Andy and asked him to bring her a copy.

She flipped the pages of the novel in her lap. After reading several chapters, Jolie had to admit Clay was a gifted writer, but why didn't he use his own name? The use of Clive Hendricks whetted her curiosity, but not enough to find him and ask him about it. Names and pseudonyms for were none of her business. She could have asked Anne, but hadn't thought of it until too late.

She'd fulfilled her obligation to help with the book signing, but hadn't decided whether or she'd attend.

Noise out in the driveway jolted her from her thoughts and speculations. Guests were arriving back from the fair. She laid aside the book, closed her computer, and hurried out to the registration desk.

One of the families clamored through the back hallway loaded down with bags. Mrs. Martin grinned at Jolie. "I've never seen so many wonderful booths at a craft fair." She held up two bags. "We bought our fair share." Two pre-teen girls flitted around their mother and darted up the stairway.

Mr. Martin came down the hall after the girls disappeared up the stairs. He carried several bags as well and stopped beside his wife. "I'm ready for a cold drink and a nap. Y'all sure know how to put on a festival or fair or whatever. The gals dragged me all over the place. Don't think we missed one booth." He kissed his wife's cheek. "See you upstairs."

"All right, honey. I have a few questions for Miss Burns." She handed him her bags. "Here, take these with you."

He grabbed them with his free hand and climbed the steps to the second floor.

Mrs. Martin leaned on the counter. "Now tell me about this handsome author everyone is talking about. I saw signs advertising a book signing next Saturday."

"That's right. Clive Hendricks is here in Weinberg and will be at Between the Pages to sign his latest book."

"Is it true he's staying here at the inn?"

The hiding out to work had definitely come to an end. "Yes, he's staying on the third floor in the suite there. I think he's at the fair now, meeting people or whatever authors do when they're out like that."

"Well, I don't read his books, but I think Don would enjoy them, so I'm going to run down to the bookstore and pick it up just so I can get him to autograph it." She hitched her purse over her shoulder. "If Don comes looking for me, tell him I'm running an errand."

With that she scurried back through the hall to the parking lot. Her mother greeted Mrs. Martin then came on to the front.

At last, her mother had returned. "I'm glad to see you're home. How did things go for the booth?"

"Just about sold out of everything. Charley and Ava Lou went back to get more plants, so I stayed with Darlene until they returned. We won't have much inventory left for tomorrow afternoon. I've never seen such big crowds before."

"That's good. You'll make a nice profit for the garden club. Now that you're here, I'm going to run out for a bit myself. Are you going to make something for supper, or should I pick up pizza or burgers?"

"I have cold cuts and soup and fruit from yesterday. Andy's going to drop by so we're good. Get yourself something if you want."

"That sounds fine for me. I'll be back about six or so." Jolie picked up the keys to her car. She had no idea exactly where she was going, but a drive around town might help her clear her thoughts about Clay.

When she drove down Main Street, she slowed as she approached the bookstore. From the looks of the people around the area, Ellie must be having a good day. Rather than risk being asked about Clay, Jolie would skip the stop here and not see Ellie. Maybe she should go back to the booth and see if they needed any help. One of the ladies was bound to need a break.

She turned into the back area where the other vendors had parked their cars and trailers, and found a spot. After locking the car, she strolled to the display area and browsed several booths as she made her way to the one manned by the garden club.

Darlene and Charley helped customers, and Ava Lou took money and charge cards and wrote receipts.

"Hi, Ava Lou. Business looks good."

She glanced up and peered over her half glasses. "Yep, Lots of people out today. Beautiful weather and good merchandise make for a profitable day. What are you doing here?"

"Oh, I thought I'd see if any of you needed a break or anything."

"I could sure use a snack about now. Lunch is long gone and it's another hour or so 'til we close." Charley's voice carried from where she collected money from a customer.

Jolie laughed, shook her head and whispered, "Should have known she'd be the first."

Charley punched her arm. "I heard that Jolene Burns, but I'll ignore it and let you get me a can or bottle of soda and something from the PTA bake sale."

"Okay, and anything for you, Ava Lou or Darlene?"

Darlene handed Ava Lou a credit card. "No, I'm fine. I have stew in the slow cooker at home, so I'll wait to eat."

Ava Lou gave Jolie a bill. "I'd like some cookies from the bake sale, but I'll stick with water to drink."

"You got it, but keep your money. Treat's on me."

"Thank you, sweetie. Oh, and by the way, Clay was by a bit ago looking for you. I told him I didn't think you were coming back today, so I don't know where he is."

"That's okay, I don't want to see him."

Ava Lou raised her eyebrows. "Why not? You two look so good together."

Charley stepped closer to hear her answer. Jolie glared at her. "Long story. I'll be back in a few." Only now she'd have to be on the look-out for Clay and avoid him no matter what.

~

With the tearoom closed today for the fair, Clay set out to find Jolie and ask her to supper. She'd stayed out of his reach all week either hiding out in her room or pretending to be too busy to talk to him and wouldn't even answer his phone calls.

Whatever had caused her to do a complete about-face on their agreement, it had been bad enough to alienate her completely. If he had hurt her in some way, he had to know how and make amends.

After searching the fairgrounds in vain, he returned to the garden club booth. Ava Lou spotted him and nudged Charley who spun around. Her face scrunched in a frown, but she waved for him to come over, but instead ran out to meet him.

"Jolie was just here. She went to get us some snacks and will be right back. She said she didn't want to see you, but I don't believe it for one minute. You two hit it off so well. Whatever happened, you gotta make it right."

"I want to, Charley, I really do, but she won't even answer my phone calls." This was one time he'd welcome some interference from these three ladies.

Darlene joined them. "I have an idea. She won't come back here if she sees you with us, so act like you're leaving and go mingle somewhere. When you see her here, hurry back, and catch her before she can leave again. We'll make some excuse so she won't leave right away."

A smile filled his heart. Trust one of them to come up with a plan. He'd thought it would be Charley, but Darlene's plan might work.

"That sounds good, so I'll walk away now in case she's watching and head for the exit then circle back." He lifted his hand in a wave. "Well, I guess I missed her again. I'll see you ladies at church tomorrow." He walked away, praying Jolie would be back.

Although he did stroll toward the exit, he managed to mingle with the crowd and make his way back behind booths in the row with the garden club. He hid behind a display and peeked around the edge. Sure enough, Jolie was in a discussion with Charley, and Ava Lou and Darlene had a customer.

Jolie stood with her back toward him when he quietly stepped up behind her.

"Hello, Jolie. I've been looking for you."

Her back stiffened, and she didn't turn around. "I thought you were gone."

He fisted his hand at his side to keep from reaching out and touching her. "Please, Jolie. Talk to me. I don't know what happened, but I thought we had a plan, an agreement."

"Just stop. I don't want to talk to you or anybody else right now." When she turned to face him, a tear trickled down her cheek. "I'm sorry, Clay. I really am." She brushed past him, but he caught her arm. She stopped, looked at his hand, then glared up at him.

Her eyes burned into his and he released his hold. This was not the time to press the issue, but he had to get her to tell him what was wrong. She marched off and disappeared into the thinning crowd now that closing time drew closer.

Darlene slipped her hand around his upper arm. "I'm so sorry, Clay. Jolene had a relationship go sour on her when she came back home to help her mom. She was dating some guy in politics, and he dropped her like a hot potato when she left him on the campaign trail. Don't know why, but she's been hiding herself away from men all these months until you came along. We had—and we still do—have high hopes for the two of you."

Ava Lou nodded and sniffed. "We're going to be praying for you two to patch up whatever it is that broke. We love Jolene like she was our own daughter, and we want to see her happy and smiling again."

People may think these women were nosy busybodies, but they had hearts of gold. If a grain of mustard seed could move a mountain, then the prayers of these ladies would open a way for him to regain Jolie's trust and friendship. He needed prayer for more than that.

"Miss Ava Lou, your prayers mean so much to me. I've only known her two weeks, but never has a woman affected me the way Jolie has. I would love to have more than friendship with her, but if that's all she's got, I'll take it."

Each of the ladies hugged him, with Charley last. "I knew there was something good about you the first time I saw you at breakfast in the tearoom. I'll talk to Emma and see what I can find out. Do you mind if I tell Emma what you said about your feelings for our Jolie?"

"No, Charley, I wouldn't mind a bit. I'd share it with the world if I thought it would do any good." Maybe he ought to at least tell Anne what had happened, and he could call his sweet, little neighbor, Mrs. Sorenson. She'd been praying for him to find someone, and now that he had, she was sure to pray even harder.

"Do any of you know what happened with my agent, Anne?" He frowned and looked around.

Charley began packing up the plants to store for the night. "Oh, she left earlier to drive back to Dallas. Said to tell you she'd see you next Saturday at the bookstore. Sure looked like she enjoyed her trip. Left with a bunch of bags and several of our plants."

"Okay, that makes sense. I'll give her a call later." He picked up a few plants. "Do you need my help with these?"

Darlene waved him off. "No, we're only going to arrange them for storage here tonight so we'll be ready after church tomorrow to open up. We might need your help at closing to get all this stuff toted home, though.

"Okay, I'll check back with you, but now I'm going to find something fast to eat and head back to the inn. I'll see you ladies in church tomorrow. Thank you again for your help and your prayers." He left them with their garden supplies and sauntered toward his car. A stop at the chicken place down the road might satisfy his physical hunger, but what was it going to take to satisfy the hunger in his heart for one innkeeper's daughter?

Chapter 13

*A*dvice, pleading, and scolding from her mother and friends wore Jolie down to a frazzle. After the tearoom closed on Wednesday, she helped her mother and Bertha clean-up. She tossed her apron into the laundry basket and turned to leave. Her mother grabbed Jolie's arm and slipped something into her pocket.

"This is a note from Clay. I want you to read it, please."

She said nothing but made a beeline for her room. Once there, she slumped on the bed and crumpled up the note. She liked Clay, but all the attention he received from others now that they knew him to be someone famous reminded her of the hurt and pain caused by Mark.

The note all but burned in the palm of her

hand, demanding to be read. She smoothed it and opened it to read.

> *"Jolie, I don't know what I've done to hurt you, but I want to make things right. We started a great friendship and had such fun outwitting your mother's friends. I should have told you my real identity, but my plans didn't include a bookstore owner who recognized me. I'm sorry if you think I was trying to deceive you. Please, let's at least be friends again. I don't want to do this book signing without you."*

The words sent guilt then anger straight to her soul. Exactly why had she avoided him? He wanted her by his side. Why? To exploit and use her to further his chances of more book sales with a local girl supporting him? *Not a chance, buster*. She planned to stay far away from the bookstore come Saturday. Business would be brisk at the tearoom, so she had an excuse for not showing up.

This time she wadded the note into a ball and tossed it toward her trash can, but it hit the rim and fell to the floor. Just like her life—never on target.

Tired of hiding out in her room, she decided to go into town for a little shopping. A new pair of shoes always lightened her mood. After a quick repair of her make-up, she grabbed up her purse and car keys. When she opened her door, she found Clay standing by the registration desk watching her door.

She slammed it shut and leaned against it. Now he stalked her so she couldn't leave her own room.

A hand pounded on her door. "Jolie, I know you're in there, so open the door and please talk to me."

"Go away and leave me alone. We have nothing to talk about." She bit her lip and willed him to disappear.

"I'm not going to leave you alone until you do talk to me. I can stand here in the lobby as long as it takes. You have to come out sometime."

The determination in his voice set her back. Now what to do? What little she did know about him reminded her Clay was a man who was accustomed to getting what he wanted, or at least that's the way she saw it.

"I'm not going away. Can't we simply talk as friends? I value your opinion about things. You have an insight few women seem to have."

What did he mean by that? Maybe he did want to be friends only, but her heart didn't see him that way, and guarding her heart took precedence over helping him.

Something pushed on the door. Jolie jumped back and her mother shoved through. "Jolie, get out there and talk to the man. I don't know what in the world happened, but whatever it was isn't worth all this moping and hiding out in your room while he roams around trying to see you."

"Mom, I can't. Mark hurt me when he broke our engagement because I wouldn't stay by his side instead of coming to help you. Even though I tried to tell him I'd be back in a month or so, he still didn't want me to come. He was selfish, arrogant, and completely unreasonable. I'm better off without him, but it still hurts. I don't want to risk my heart again."

Mom fisted her hands on her hips. "Good grief, sweetie, who said anything about risking your heart. Sure, the girls and I hoped for more, but now we'd like to see you be at least friends again. Think of all the fun at church and driving out in the country. That doesn't have to change."

"But Mom, I started caring more about him as more than a friend. It can't ever be more than that because he'll be leaving and going back to his world and forgetting all about me." Jolie fought the tears welling in her eyes. She covered them with her hands.

"Sweetie, I know this is hard." Mom wrapped her arms around Jolie. "But why don't you give him a chance? Talk to him and help us with the book signing. Emma has made wonderful plans with signs all over town advertising the appearance of Clive Hendrix at her store. If you still feel the same after that, then let us know and we'll leave you two alone to do whatever you want to do."

What Mom said made sense, but getting the

heart to cooperate involved more than Jolie wanted to face at the moment. Still, she must talk with him at some point. He'd be here another month or so, and avoiding him became more difficult every day.

"All right, I'll talk to him, but give me a few to wash my face." No way would she let him see the tear stains.

Mom left and after a few minutes, her face washed, make-up repaired, and emotions in check, Jolie opened the door and stepped into the foyer. Clay stood near the desk and he didn't move toward her. He wasn't going to make this easy. She stopped a few feet away. "Okay, you want to talk, let's talk."

~

Clay hooked his fingers into the back pockets of his jeans. His heart started pounding the moment Mrs. Burns told him Jolie agreed to meet him. When her door opened, he jumped and his throat all but closed.

No expression, no emotion, nothing in her eyes or face gave him a clue as to what to do. "I'm not sure where to start." He hesitated seeking the right words. "Something happened last week after you found out I'm a writer."

"Not just *any* writer. You're Clive Hendrix."

He frowned, then shook his head. "So that makes a difference?"

"Of course it does. I've seen how people crowd around you now and bring their books to be autographed and take pictures with you." She crossed her arms over her chest.

"They're fans, and some of them probably don't even read my books. They buy them for the autographs, and may even sell them on E-bay after that. Those books make me a living. I'm not a John Grisham, David Baldacci, or Tom Clancy. They're the famous ones." Who in the world did she think he was? He was nowhere near the celebrity those men were.

She shook her head. "Stop, I don't even know who those men are, and I don't care."

"Jolene, we had fun the first two weeks, and the day we went out to see the bluebonnets when I told you the truth. I hoped that kiss would mean something to you, but everything changed. I want it back like it was before. Can't we be friends?"

She blinked her eyes several times like she was holding back tears. "I don't know, Clay."

When she spoke, he had to lean forward to hear her.

"I guess you weren't really trying to fool me," she continued. "But it was such a surprise to find out you are a celebrity. I've had enough of those to last a life-time."

"Is that what your breakup was all about?" At her startled expression, he quickly added, "Your mom wouldn't give me any details except that you'd been hurt by someone before you moved in with her. I'm sorry about the breakup, but in a way, glad. If you'd stayed in Houston, I would never have met you, and that would have been my loss."

She bit her lip and kept her head down. "I'm not sure what to do right now. Give me more time to think about things."

His heart warmed at her words. She'd think about it and that was good enough for now. "I'll give you all the time you need. Believe me when I say I would never do anything to hurt you. I care about you, your mother, and this inn. No matter what you decide, I *will* stay here for the time I reserved the room." And even longer if that's it would take to win her trust and her heart.

"Thank you. My mind is in confusion and turmoil and I can't think straight. I'll . . .I'll let you know something before Saturday." With that she retreated back to her room and closed the door.

Clay slumped against the wall and blew out his breath. That didn't go like he wanted, but better than he'd thought it might. He had no idea what she meant by having enough of celebrities? He sure wasn't one although he had become one in this small town.

No matter what others thought, Jolene was the only one whose opinion meant anything. He straightened. No time to think about those things now. He still had a deadline.

However, once he reached his room and sat down at the computer, the only image to come to his mind was that of Jolene Burns. Frustrated, he rose and stood by the windows giving him a view of the garden below and the fields beyond. Blue-purple flowers covered the fields in a blanket of color that dazzled his eyes and filled his heart with love.

Love? He nodded . . . Yes . . . love for Jolie grew stronger every time she came near. He so had wanted to grab her and hold her in his arms downstairs, but then she might have pushed him away forever.

Someone knocked on his door. "Clay, it's Mrs. Burns. May I speak with you?"

He hurried to the door and opened it. "What is it? Has something happened?"

"No, no, nothing's happened. I just wanted you to know how much Andy and I like you and want to help you with Jolie. It's her trust that has to be won because deep down I think she cares for more you much more than she's admitting to anyone, even herself."

"I appreciate that, but I don't see it. All I see is distrust and uncertainty. I don't know the details of her breakup with her last boyfriend, and I don't need to know unless she wants to tell me herself."

"That's good, and I believe she will eventually. The thing you need to do now is to regain her trust. Andy and I will help with that. I'll keep my friends out of this. They want to do their part, but sometimes they do more harm than good." She hugged him then stepped back. "I hope you don't mind the hug. You're a good man, Clayton Hill, and I'd be proud to have you dating my daughter."

She didn't wait for a response and left Clay

standing in the doorway with his mouth open. He sure hadn't expected anything like that. He didn't mind the hug at all. In fact, it made him a little homesick for his mom right now. He breathed deeply, exhaled, and returned to his desk. Several things now stood in his favor. Mrs. Sorenson, Mrs. Burns, and all her friends prayed for him and his relationship with Jolene.

God listened to the prayers of His children, and Clay added his own for God to answer all their prayers with a positive response from Jolie. Time to stop worrying, leave it with the Lord, and get back on track to finding more problems and dangers for his hero. His fingers clicked on the keys and words flew onto the screen.

Chapter 14

*B*y Friday afternoon, Jolie's emotions calmed enough for her to make the decision to be at the book signing. As hard as it might be, she would make sure Ellie had a successful event at her store. Not that Ellie needed any assistance from Jolie, but showing support would the better thing to do for Mom's friend.

Afterward, with her emotions under control, she went in search of Clay, but before she got very far, Anne showed up to register for the week-end. "Hello, Mrs. Holcomb. Welcome to Bluebonnet Inn."

"Oh, Jolie, call me Anne. All my friends do, and I hope we will be friends."

Jolie pushed the registration form across the counter. "We still do some things the old-fashioned way, so if you'll sign your name and your license plate number, we'll be all set.

After signing her name, Anne laid down the pen and peered up at Jolie. "Have you talked to Clay yet?"

The question sent Jolie's heart to spinning. How did Anne know they hadn't been speaking? "I was just looking for him when you came in."

"What happened, Jolie? Clay told me about you and how much he enjoyed being with you. That's not like him. He rarely has much to do with women and seldom if ever dates. He's dedicated to his work and says he doesn't have time for distractions."

"Then why is he pursuing me like this. I can't . . ." She hesitated. "He's leaving in a month and I'll never see him again."

Anne reached for Jolie's hands. "Honey, he's fallen head over heels for you. I can hear it in his voice when he talks about you and I saw it in his eyes last week."

A lump formed in her throat, and Jolie swallowed hard. She wanted to believe Anne, but a man like Clay didn't need a small-town girl. He needed someone who could be in the spotlight and support him in all that he did. An idea flitted through her mind. *I could do that.* What was she really afraid of? Moisture filled her eyes and she blinked.

"Anne, I'm so confused right now. I was looking for Clay to tell him I'd be at the book signing tomorrow, but now I'm not so sure. I have a few things to think about." That wasn't true. She'd been thinking the past two days. Why was she undecided? Why couldn't she simply trust Clay and enjoy the time they had left of his stay?

Anne dug into her purse and pulled out her phone. "You know, if you two did get together, he might even stay here. Let me call him." She swiped her fingers across the screen and tapped on a number. "Here, you talk to him." She held the phone out to Jolie.

"I . . . I don't know." Jolie bit her lip, but let Anne place it in her hand. Clay's voice came over the phone. "Hello, Anne? Are you here?"

She held it up to her ear. "Uh, it's Jolie. Anne gave me her phone."

"Jolie? Does this mean you're talking to me again?"

"I was looking for you when Anne came in to register."

"I'm on my way down." Footsteps pounded on the stairway and seconds later Clay appeared at the landing.

Chill bumps big as hen eggs covered her arms. Frozen to the spot, Jolie said nothing but handed the phone back to Anne. After a moment of silence, she said, "Hello, Clay."

He descended the remainder of the stairway and stopped at the bottom. "I'm here. Please tell me you'll be at the bookstore tomorrow."

She stared into the brown eyes that had

charmed her the first day of his arrival. His hair stood on end as if he'd raked his hands through it, and he wore faded jeans and a Texas Rangers t-shirt. Her heart rate raced into double time as she nodded her head.

Anne grinned, picked up her key and headed for the stairs. "I'll see you two later."

Clay moved closer. "That's the prettiest nod I've ever seen. I've missed you this week. No plotting or planning or thinking we're fooling the ladies."

The smile she'd held back for a week came now. "Yeah, I sorta missed you, too."

"Does this mean we're friends again? We can go out for pizza or burgers and fries and have fun like we did before?"

Jolie laughed. "Don't know about burgers and fries, but pizza sounds good." Movement to her right caught her eye. She looked that way to find her mother and Bertha peering around the door. Her mother gave Jolie a thumbs-up approval.

"Mom!" Then she laughed and shook her head. "Come on out. You've been caught."

"I'm sorry dear, but we couldn't help but overhear. We didn't want to interrupt or anything." Mom grinned then wrapped her arms around Clay's chest. "I'm so happy"

Anne descended the steps and approached Jolie's mom. "Hi, Mrs. Burns." She linked arms with Mom. "It's about time these two were speaking again. It's been a long week."

"Tell me about it. Jolie hiding away in her room and Clay trying every way he could think of to get her attention. It's been a real doozy."

The two women giggled and laughed like schoolgirls.

"Mom, we're right here you know."

"Oh yes, I do know." She patted Jolie's arm. "Now what do you say we get cleaned up and have supper?" I have a huge pan of lasagna cooking, garlic bread, and a big salad waiting for us. Dinner will be ready in twenty minutes, so chop, chop, and do what you have to do."

"Then I'm outta here. Going home to take care of my man." Bertha grinned and headed for the door.

Jolie shrugged and turned to Clay. "I guess I'll see you for supper."

Clay reached out and pulled her to him in a hug. "I'm so glad you're not angry with me anymore. Don't know why you were, and at the moment, I don't really care. This is going to be the longest twenty minutes." He released her and bounded up the stairway, whistling as he went.

Jolie slumped against the desk. Either she'd just made the biggest mistake of her life or she was going to have the best weekend in years. She preferred the latter.

~

The next morning, Clay sat at the table Ellie placed off to one side of the bookstore. Last night had been a bust. After dinner, new guests checking in kept Jolie busy, and Anne wanted to go over his manuscript, so they'd had no time together. Jolie promised to be at the bookstore this morning when the signing began, but so far she hadn't shown up.

Anne spread more bookmarks across the table. "Don't look so glum. She'll be here. The store's been open only half an hour and you've already signed nearly a dozen books. Who knew there'd be that many readers of your books in this town?"

"I'm surprised, too, but Ellie said a lot of people at the fair told her they'd be back this week." He'd rather have Jolie sitting in the empty chair beside him for the next two hours.

"Good morning, Clay. Care to sign my book for me?" Andy Benefield handed Clay a copy of the book. "I bought it here when it first came out. As I said, I'm a fan."

"Happy to sign it for you. Did you meet Anne last week at the fair?"

"Yes, I did. Good to see you again." He moved to the end of the table to speak with her.

"Have many customers?" Jolie slid onto the chair beside him.

Clay's heart jumped then went into a rhythm that caught his breath. "You made it."

Today she wore khaki slacks and a blue knit top that matched her eyes which had become his favorite color this week. Her hair hung loose in waves about her shoulders, and it was all he could do to keep from pushing it back from her face and cupping her cheek in his hand.

"I said I would, and I'm a woman of my word." Her smile lit up her face and eyes filled with the sparkle he'd missed so much the past week.

A customer handed him a book, which brought him back to his purpose for being there. His already pounding heart spiraled in a tail spin that made him forget what he was doing. He stared at the blank space a moment then blinked his eyes. His name. He had to sign his name. Clay picked up the black marker and signed his pen name on the title page.

The woman smiled broadly and hugged the book to her chest. "My husband loves your books. This one is for his birthday."

After she left, a steady stream of people lined up at the table to have books signed. Some were the latest one, but a number of them were older copies as well. Where had all these people come from? Ellie told him she sent fliers to neighboring towns, but this number far exceeded his expectations.

The crowd thinned just before finishing time. Clay leaned back with a satisfied sigh. "My one big fear is to have a signing where no one shows up, and I've had a few of those before."

Ellie appeared at the table, her face glowing with happiness. "This has been marvelous. A lot of people had your book already, but most bought something else while they were here. Thank you so much for doing this for the store."

"You're welcome, Ellie. You and your friends have been very kind. I'm glad it was a success." He sensed Jolie standing beside him.

"You don't have to leave now, do you?" He had so much he still wanted to say to her but not here.

"It's noon and Mom will need help with the tearoom. We can get together after that."
Andy shook his head. "No, Anne and I agreed to go back and help your mom. You two go have lunch somewhere."

"There, you're free. Please say you'll come with me." He'd never had to plead with women to go anywhere with him or even to talk with him, but Jolie had him tied in knots he wanted to get unraveled right away.

"I guess I can't say no."

"Thanks, Andy, Anne. I owe you two." He grabbed Jolie's hand and led her outside. Once they were in his car, he reached for her hands. "I have so much I want to say to you, but not here, and I don't want to go to the tearoom or diner. They're too noisy."

"We can go to the park or the gazebo first."

"Perfect. The gazebo it is." He started the car and pulled out of the parking spot. Hunger could wait.

~

Jolie's head spun with all the things she wanted to say to him, and her heart thumped within her chest. She wanted more than friendship, but it was too soon. She hadn't known him long enough for love, and she couldn't risk being hurt again. If they could be friends and enjoy each other's company for the rest of his stay, she'd be content and settle for that.

Five minutes later, Clay parked the car at the rear of the inn. He came around and opened the door for her. She stepped out of the car and stood. Clay positioned himself so close to her that his breath brushed her cheek. His eyes held such intensity her breath caught and her nerves tied themselves into a knot in the pit of her stomach.

Jolie stepped aside to take a deep breath and pointed to the empty gazebo. She pulled his hand. "No one's in the gazebo. Let's go."

Once they were seated on the bench, Jolie's voice left her. Everything she wanted to say lodged somewhere deep inside. The sun shone through the trees casting lacy leaf shadows across Clay's face and warming her shoulders. How could she ever let him go?

He grasped her hands again. "Jolie, I don't know why or how you were hurt in the past, but I want you to know I would never do anything to hurt you because I care too much about you. We've known each other only a few weeks, but in that time, I've come to know enough about you to want to spend more time with you."

"But you have a book to write. You're here to work." Jolie wanted to slap herself. Such a dumb, obvious statement to make.

"Yes, but it'll never get written if you shut me out of your life like you have the past week."

He leaned closer and Jolie's mouth became as dry as West Texas sand. "I...I don't ...I don't know—what to say."

He leaned closer, his whisper a breath in her ears. "Then don't say anything." One hand cupped her cheek, and the other brushed back a stray strand of hair. He kissed her neck just below her ear then his lips found hers. His touch, soft at first, became harder and deeper.

Caution flew off in the breeze and Jolie returned his kiss with all of her heart. Their first kiss had been light and in the spirit of the moment, but this one unleashed the all the joy and love she'd bottled up the past months. Her arms went around his neck and her fingers tangled in his hair.

When they parted, they sat with foreheads together, savoring the moment.

"Jolie, you've opened up a part of me I've kept closed off for too long. Please don't close it again."

"I won't. I trust you and whatever it takes to make this work, I'm willing to do." She pulled back to stare into his eyes. The glow coming from them heightened her desire and underscored the love growing for him in her heart and soul.

He kissed her again and again. After the third one, he stopped, shook his head and laughed. "Just imagine what the ladies will do with this. You think they'll be surprised?"

Jolie grinned and placed her fingertips on his

lips. "Not surprised but beside themselves with joy and 'I told you so'. Let them have their fun, but I'm going to enjoy the ride, and see where it takes us."

God had a plan for her after all. This is why she had returned to Weinberg and the Bluebonnet Inn.

The End

Check out other stories in the American Flowers collection:

Sweet Apple Blossom

Magnolia Lane

Hawthorne Hope

Apple Blossom Daze

Maine's White Pine Cone Conspiracy

Wild Prairie Rose

Love's Violet Sunrise

Forget Me Not

Six Little Sunflowers

Orange Blossom Cafe

ABOUT THE AUTHOR

Martha Rogers is a free-lance writer and was named Writer of the Year at the Texas Christian Writers Conference in 2009 and writes a weekly devotional for ACFW. Martha and her husband Rex live in Houston where they enjoy spending time with their grandchildren. A former English and Home Economics teacher, Martha loves to cook and experimenting with recipes and loves scrapbooking when she has time. She has written three series, *Winds Across the Prairie* and *Seasons of the Heart and The Homeward Journey.* Book three in that series, *Love Never Fails,* released in November, 2014.

Check out other great Forget Me Not Romances and sign up for our newsletter at
www.forgetmenotromances.com

Social Media:
Facebook: Martha L. Rogers
Twitter: @MarthaRogers2
Website: www.marthawrogers.com
Pinterest: www.pinterest.com/grammymartha/

Love in the Bayou City of Texas:
Love on Trial
Forgiving Love

River Walk Christmas
Best Laid Plans
Not on the Menu

Series:
Winds Across the Prairie: **The Homeward**
Journey

Becoming Lucy   *Love Stays True*
Morning for Dove   *Love Finds Faith*
Finding Becky   *Love Never Fails*
Caroline's Choice
Amelia's Journey
Christmas at Holly Hill
Seasons of the Heart
Summer Dream
Autumn Song
Winter Promise
Spring Hope

Made in the USA
Monee, IL
14 March 2020